WYLDE SWIMMING

By Simon Tozer

ISBN: 9798354786428
First Published 2022.
First Edition.

www.devonauthor.co.uk

Author photo by Poppy Jakes
Copy Editing by Becky Jones

PROLOGUE

23rd May 1921 - Lemoncombe Beach, South Devon

A lone man sat on the sandstone rocks on the beach and gazed out to sea. He looked to be in his forties, his fair hair windswept from the sea breeze His outfit was casual - an Argyle sweater and white linen trousers.

He watched intently as the cormorants dived for fish, the sunlight playing on the ripples that they formed in the azure sea.

There was no one else on the beach, so he was able to sit with his own thoughts, remembering a time when he was not alone. In the past, he and his wife, Doris, would come and sit here, delighting in watching the sea birds, the seals and the occasional school of dolphins swim by.

Doris was no longer around, having died a couple of years ago, but he still returned to sit on the beach and contemplate better times.

He was a very positive man and he still took delight in seeing the wonders of nature in this beautiful location at Lemoncombe Beach. But despite his optimism, he could not see an obvious way in which his future would progress.

Of course he was totally unaware of Olivia and the part she would play in his future. That was all yet to come.

CHAPTER ONE

Sunday 28th November 2021 – Lemoncombe Beach

There were four of us ladies and, as per usual, they parked at my house and we all headed down to the beach together with our various bags slung over our shoulders.
Suze and Linda were already wearing their "dry robes" like many others heading down to the beach.

Bren and I were just wearing our coats against the cool air, our dry robes tucked away inside our bags. I say "dry robes" but being honest most of them aren't actually from that particular brand, which has become as synonymous with an item of clothing as "Hoover" was with vacuum cleaners or "Google" with searching on the Internet.

"Olivia," Suze called over her shoulder. "What boots are you wearing today?"

I replied, "I've got my wetsuit socks with my strap up blue boots. I find they keep my feet warm but also keep most of the water out. If I wear the boots without the socks, the boots fill up with water. If I wear the socks without the boots, they slip down." The other three laughed gently as we made our way on to the steep steps heading down past the café to the beach.

Suze and Linda fell into an easy conversation about hats. Suze had decided to wear her strap-on orange and black neoprene hat, while Linda had brought her 1970s style yellow floral hat. My winter hat was similar to the one worn by Suze, whereas Bren, who refused to get her hair wet, always wore her famous bobble hat!

The café was open, promoting hot chocolate and cake on the chalkboard that stood outside the door, already serving grateful swimmers, walkers and others sitting out on the balcony enjoying the cool winter sunshine and the gentle sound of the waves.

The beach was already surprisingly full, the outline of bodies spread out across the dark red sands. The cliffs surrounding the beach were a mixture of the same dark red sandstone and greenery, where trees and shrubs clung precipitously to the cliff faces. The sun shone on the blue sea and one could easily be forgiven for thinking that they were on a Greek island, at least until they felt that bracing Northerly breeze.

The storm from the previous day had shifted the sands yet again, making it difficult to clamber over the rocks to finally reach the beach, but we managed it without too much difficulty or loss of dignity. Behind us, a couple in their sixties seemed to be having more difficulty, the lady in question seemed to take an age, not just because she was particular about where she could stand, but also because she felt the need to pause often and shout at her husband for all the beach to hear.

We said hello to a few other fellow swimmers on the beach as we got ready. Some had already been for their swim and were either reclining in the morning sun sipping their warm drinks or were getting changed and trying not to get too much sand inside their socks.
Others, like us, were just arriving or getting ready to swim.

Swimming at the end of November in the sea in the UK?

Were we crazy?

Just two years earlier, when our story started, I would never have dreamt of swimming in the sea in September, let alone November. The cafe wouldn't have been open. No-one had heard of Covid-19. Very few people ever wore a face mask and even fewer knew what 'social distancing' or 'lockdown' were. For myself, I had never heard of Dry Robes, neoprene hats or Elm House. Nor could I ever have imagined what was about to happen to me...

CHAPTER TWO

Thursday 28th November 2019 – Haldon Hill, South Devon

The name I was given at my christening was Olivia Wylde. My parents were actually considering calling me Oscar if I was a boy. Fortunately for me, I wasn't a boy and they plumped for Olivia instead of the awful Oscarina...yes, they were really considering that at one point.

I have spent around four decades explaining that it is Wylde with a "Y" and an "E" and still having people spell it incorrectly. More recently there had been the added confusion of an actress named "Olivia Wilde", so when people said to me "Oh, like the actress?" I just nodded and put up with the erroneous letter "I".

I had just turned 45, my birthday being exactly one week earlier on the 21st November. Apparently this made me on the cusp of being a Scorpio and a Sagittarius, though I had no idea what that meant.

I'd been in a long term relationship with John Martin for over twenty years but we did not have any children. John always wanted children but I was no longer able to conceive after a bad miscarriage some fifteen years previously. It was something that still came up when we were arguing, hurling words at each other, each one aimed to hurt. John had always blamed me for the fact that we didn't have children, without even considering how it hurt me.

Our lack of children meant that we've both had time to spend on other things. John was an accountant but seemed to spend more time on the golf course than anywhere else. A few years ago I qualified and started practising as a Bowen therapist, working with humans and animals. If you don't know what that is, a fellow practitioner used to call it “chiropracty without the crunch!”. Basically I treated humans and horses (yes horses) with a number of small movements to help their bodies repair themselves. If anyone ever doubted it worked and blamed it on some people who will believe anything, I would always point to the horses and say “yes I am pulling the wool over their eyes too!”.

I also spent a lot of time in our garden, growing flowers and shrubs, as well as a wide range of fruit and vegetables. We were practically self-sufficient in vegetables, which was handy seeing as I was vegetarian. John wasn't vegetarian but, as he never did the cooking, he tended to eat what I prepared which was largely vegetarian, though I did prepare some meat and fish dishes for him on occasion.

I had a big love for 1980s music and films, especially if the women had very big hair. I also had a nostalgia for things before my time, classic black and white British movies with Dennis Price or Noel Coward talking terribly, terribly nicely or Alastair Sim bringing Terry Thomas down to size. My favourite author was Agatha Christie and the fact that her house was just down the road at Greenway always gave me pleasure. I loved to find the subtle and sometimes unsubtle references to local places in her stories. I always dreamed that one day John would take me to Burgh Island, so that I could wallow in some Agatha Christie related nostalgia but i was still waiting.

We had a lovely house in the countryside in South Devon and both had good friends around us. My main hobbies were Pilates, followed by a swim and steam room at the local leisure centre, and maintaining the garden of course, whereas John was into golf and cars. However we both enjoyed a good walk together in the Devon countryside. Who wouldn't? We were blessed with some of the best scenery in the UK.

So this was our life together. In the last few years, John and I had become slightly more distant but there was never any inkling of a break up and, despite the fact that he was sometimes ungrateful and uncaring, I had no thought about us ever splitting up.

Being my own boss, I was able to take some time off during the week. During my birthday week, I took a day off and the girls joined me for a walk on Dartmoor followed by a late birthday lunch at one of the pubs.

Jillian lived with her husband, Adam, who was a top doctor at the local hospital. Because of this, Jillian was able to not work and look after their home. She spent a lot of her time running the local WI, and other groups in town, so being a housewife worked for her.

Suze was unmarried, but we loved to hear about her latest dating escapades, and she never failed to disappoint. She, like John, was an accountant, but they worked for different companies, and dealt with very different types of client. She was gorgeous, with dark nut brown skin, and her tall, athletic frame putting us all to shame.

Bren was my oldest friend, and we had known each other for over twenty years. She was married to Keith and had worked every job under the sun. She was stunningly beautiful and still turned heads wherever she went. She was a few years older than all of us but you wouldn't believe it to look at her. She took part in everything but was always dressed inadequately. On our walk across the Tors of Dartmoor, we had all sensibly opted for walking boots, but Bren had decided on trainers, which quickly became caked in mud.

"Bren, why do you never wear the right footwear?" Said Suze.

"At least she has taken off her high heels!" Laughed Jillian.

"Oh, leave her alone. At least she's here and trying," I said, before realising how patronising my comment sounded.

Bren, however, was barely paying attention. She was tilting her face up to enjoy the warm November sunshine. It was one of those days when you felt quite mild in the sunshine and then you went into the shade and it felt bloody freezing.

Dartmoor looked fabulous on those days, the sun shining, the sky bright and clear, and hardly a soul walking around. The granite outcrops looked like giant fingers pushing up through the grass.

The path made its way through some old, gnarled trees and then we came across a couple of deep, dark pools. The sun glittered on the heather around them but the water seemed to absorb the sun completely.

"Oh wow," said Suze. "They look so tempting."

"Don't be daft, woman," said Jillian. "They look absolutely, terrifyingly cold."

"Well, there's only one way to find out," said Suze, as she started to remove her clothing.

We were astonished. We knew that Suze was into what people now called "wild swimming". I knew she would swim once a week in the sea, wearing a range of protective garments but to strip off to her undies in the middle of Dartmoor at the end of November, surely not!

She was already down to her underwear and looked around her. "Are you coming in, Olivia?"

The mere suggestion seemed crazy, but part of me was wondering what it would be like.

Suze continued to stand there half naked before the three of us. She didn't worry about modesty and to be honest, her body was very well toned.

She looked at me again questioningly, though for some reason she did not try and persuade the other two. However I just stood there, not knowing what to do.

"Oh well, your loss," she said as she walked gingerly into the nearest pool.

"Oh fucking hell, it's cold!" she cried.

She didn't stop though and soon her whole body was submersed in the dark water. The pool was only about 15 metres from one side to the other, so Suze did a couple of widths of breaststroke and backstroke. She then rose from the water and we all stared at her perfect body as the water dripped off her.

She noticed us and said, "See, I knew you lot were on the turn."

We all laughed and she tried to dry herself off with her shift. Fortunately she was not one for miniscule items of clothing but the garment she used was still inadequate for the job, so I handed over my thick scarf to help as the goose pimples spread over her body.

"How did it feel?"

"Amazing," she replied and then she just stood there while the November sun spread over her body.

I suddenly felt very jealous of her and wished I had tried to go in too but the moment had passed. Suze got dressed, placed the squeezed undies in her coat pocket and we headed off on the rest of our walk to make for the pub.

CHAPTER THREE

I carried on swimming with the ladies twice a week at the pool in Newton Abbot. Suze carried on "wild swimming" outside once a week, she mainly went in the sea as she told us it was warmer in the sea in November and December than it was in April but none of us believed her. We all thought she was mad.

Christmas came and went. John had outdone himself on the present front. I wish I could have said that he had surprised me with buying me something unexpected but amazing, but no. What he had decided to buy me as my main gift was a set of ladies golf clubs. I had never shown any interest in playing golf and he knew it wasn't my thing but he still bought them for me and thought he was being creative.

He explained, "I was getting myself a new hybrid..." whatever that was "...when I saw this ladies set in the sale and I thought, that would be perfect for Liv. Get her into golf and we can go together then. Stop you moaning about me disappearing for the day!"

So that was it, he wanted me to join him, so he didn't feel so guilty. I knew another reason was that he wanted me to drive so that he could get pissed!

Not the best present ever. Unsurprisingly I never used it and he felt I was being ungrateful and made a big hoo-ha about having to sell it on Ebay, and then didn't even bother to get me anything with the money he made from the sale.

Oh well. It went along with the scarf he bought me which was the same as the one he had bought me the year before and I'd never worn, the scented candles which were full of awful chemicals or the quite tacky jewellery which looked like it should be worn in a pantomime.

I'm sorry if I sounded a bit ungrateful but he never put any thought into his gifts and was more interested in the new car he had bought himself with this year's tax earnings.

I popped around to Suze's house on Christmas Day. We had both been invited around for Christmas dinner but John had said no. I decided to head around later for the post dinner fun but went alone as John said he had no interest in going at all. Suze was with her latest partner Christie. Christie didn't seem right for Suze, therefore I wasn't too surprised when they split up a month or so later.

On Christmas Day I was made welcome and did enjoy the company and chatting but I felt guilty about leaving John on his own alone on Christmas Day, therefore in the early evening I made my excuses and returned home to find John playing with his computer console on the television. He barely grunted as I tried to chat, as he was too busy killing aliens or Americans or whatever it was he did on there. Dispirited, I headed off for an early night to bring to an end a slightly mournful Christmas Day.

On Boxing Day I had arranged with some of the girls to join the charity run into the sea at Teignmouth. We were raising money for the RNLI, which was obviously a great cause but I was sure there were some better, warmer and drier ways of donating.

John was heading off to play a charity golf tournament, so I drove over on my own, dreading it the whole way. It actually wasn't as bad as I thought it was going to be. There were literally hundreds of people gathered on the beach,and most of them were doing the sea dip.

I wore red leggings and a sweatshirt along with my Santa hat.

Like most people I just ran into the sea, splashed about for a bit and then got out again. Whereas Suze, who was just wearing her swimming costume and a Santa hat, stayed in the sea, swimming around happily. She got some appreciative glances from a group of men.

Suze, Bren and I went back to my house afterwards to warm up. I had pre-made some mushroom soup, which we re-heated and ate with toast. After overdoing it the day before with food and drink, the cold water followed by the soup was just what we all needed.

A few days later, the news reported about a new SARS virus somewhere in China but most of us paid little attention. We had heard it all before and nothing had happened. Life carried on as normal.

Again New Year was a bit of a disappointment. We went around to a friend's house for a big party but it was obvious she was trying to set me up with an estate agent friend of her husband, despite the fact that I was with John. “Oh, I thought the two of you had split up some time ago.” she said.

“No, he's over there,” I replied, pointing at John talking to another couple.

“Oh, well strange I’m not sure why I thought that, anyway what a shame, Leslie would have been a good match for you.”

Leslie had seemed like a nice enough chap but we had nothing to chat about and he got confused and moved away when I explained I was vegetarian.

I don't know if it is the fact that I don't eat meat or that being vegetarian might be indicative of other alternative tendencies that might scare off some of the more conservative men I met. Maybe they think that I might start spouting Trotskyist propaganda or burn my bra or something like that. Either that or they didn't find me attractive...heaven forbid!

It did annoy me slightly, even though I was obviously not on the pull, that I didn't have the pulling power of Bren or Suze.

In the middle of January, we had all heard a bit more about the SARS virus which they were now referring to as "Coronavirus" and the first death which had occurred in China. Still, we did nothing and thought it would not affect us, just like all the other viruses like this before it.

Over the next couple of weeks, the news about Coronavirus began to seep more and more into our news. The first cases outside China were found. The Chinese closed down the city of Wuhan and we watched disturbing footage of empty streets and medical staff in full body suits. But again, we knew that kind of thing couldn't happen over here.

Then the first actual deaths happened outside of China, while the death toll rose steadily there. The WHO declared a global health emergency and we all started to pay more attention. A cruise liner called the Diamond Princess had a major outbreak and passengers had to stay on board. People travelling in from China to the UK had to quarantine. In February, the virus was given a new name that would stay on everyone's lips for months to come, Covid 19.

We started being a bit more cautious out and about but still carried on life as just before. Even in March things were carrying on much as before but things were slowly starting to change. I went along to a business breakfast networking event at Teignmouth Golf Club on the 12th March and there were over forty people there. People were beginning to talk more and more about this thing called "social distancing". People tried this new idea of tapping foot to foot instead of shaking hands but this made other people laugh at the silliness of it all.

Other people spoke about how some business events had been

cancelled or postponed as people started to stay at home rather than go to meetings and therefore not enough people were interested in going. This group, however, was fairly full and we all sat around tables together and chatted, stood together for photos and apart from not shaking hands, not much was very different than before.

Then things began to change. First came the stockpiling. People fought in supermarket aisles over the last packet of toilet rolls. Within weeks there seemed to be a national shortage of loo rolls and whenever some fresh stock was delivered to a shop they disappeared from the shelves in minutes. Perhaps people were shitting themselves in fear?!

On the 16th March Boris announced that we should stop non-essential travel. The Government were also clear that we could see our way out of this if we all worked together, the virus would come and go and we would return to normal in a few months. But even so, some people were shocked at the idea of this dragging on for more than a couple of weeks.

Then a new word came into the British vocabulary, "lockdown". Everyone was talking about whether there would be a lockdown or not. Would Boris risk it? Would he not? Whatever happened we knew we just had to get to the summer and it would all pass, just like the flu...

Finally on the 23rd March the Government announced the first lockdown, this came into force on the 26th March, who knew what would happen next?

CHAPTER FOUR

The start of lockdown hit me badly. My work stopped completely, so not only was I stuck at home but I had nothing to take my mind off it. John as an accountant was suddenly busier than ever, as he had to help his clients (rather grudgingly if he was honest about it) work out what to do. He was grumpier than ever and barely spoke to me for weeks.

I decided to do what I could around the house and garden. The weather was very good so it was a great time to make changes. I started ordering things on the internet and the first job I did was to tidy up the flower beds by the wall and give that a new lick of masonry paint. Having done a good job on that, I decided to do the same with the two sheds, the wood store and the wooden fence. I ordered two different colours of paint online and came up with a modern looking style and pattern. So effective was it that it looked like everything was brand new rather than a bit old and tired.

I brought John out to see the changes I had made and see what he thought, but he barely looked and only grunted in acknowledgement. I let him go as I knew he was working hard.

We were only allowed to leave the house for essential shopping and for one bit of exercise per day. Therefore I decided to take a daily walk. I started with heading towards Haldon Hill near where we lived but that entailed walking on a couple of main roads to get to the nicer parts, so I also tried heading down the hill and investigating all the lanes in and around Teignmouth and nearby areas that I could reach on foot, finding some places I never knew existed. This was the highlight of lockdown for me in March and April 2020.

Although I felt that the lockdown was bad for me, I was still lucky. I had a great house, a great garden that I could work on and lovely walks in and around the area. We were very lucky in Devon, not only did we have great countryside around us but the rates of Covid down here were minimal compared with some parts of the country.

One thing that John and I did agree on, was the daily watching of the news. We actually took to watching the six o'clock news on BBC, followed by the local Spotlight news afterwards and then we would often watch a bit of the Channel 4 news too, as it often went more in depth. Soon we had started skipping the six o'clock news and just watched the local news and the Channel 4 news.

And the news was harrowing. While the local news was talking mainly about businesses, local travel restrictions and the number of cases, the national news was telling us about the hospitalisations and deaths, the worried family members who could not visit their loved ones, the people who were starting to die in care homes.

Then a new phrase came into our lexicon, PPE. Could the hospitals get enough PPE? Did we need PPE ourselves? Were the army going to help deliver PPE? If there was a worldwide shortage of PPE, how was more going to get where it was needed? What did PPE actually stand for?

My car stayed in the garage and I didn't drive for weeks, just like so many other people. Whether it was imagined or not, the air definitely seemed clearer and there did seem more birds and animals out and about when I went walking. The noise levels were definitely reduced. As I walked around the lanes, I was almost deafened by the lack of car and business noise. You could hear birds sing, the wind blow in the trees and the crashing of waves on the beach. There were also so many people walking, as they were not allowed to travel and everyone was friendly to each other, though none of us would get very close.

For many it was like an extra holiday in the sun and a chance to investigate their local area, in a way that many had forgotten. If it hadn't been a time of illness and death, I am sure some people would have looked back at those early weeks of Covid as halcyon days of idyll and simple pleasures.

March turned into April. Prince Charles and Boris Johnson had caught Covid, which brought it home to even more people, making everyone realise that anyone could get it. Despite the lockdown, Dominic Cummings drove over 250 miles to Durham with his wife and child. The media called for his resignation but No.10 did nothing, which annoyed the public even more.

As we weren't able to meet up in person, the girls and I arranged a regular meet up on a video chat. It took us a little while to work it all out. When we first did it, only two of us managed to get online and even then getting our audio and video to work was a nightmare. By the third meeting we had six of us but Bren still couldn't manage to coordinate getting her audio working and appearing the right way around (her video was sideways). We tried to explain to her that she needed to turn her tablet around but it still didn't work.

On the third meeting, as well as drinking, we arranged a quiz which actually turned out to be more fun than we thought. It was one of Suze's swimming pals who suggested it. Apparently she and her family were doing online quizzes and having a great time. As I had no immediate family left, there were no family video calls to arrange, so enjoying it with the girls was a blessing.

As the weeks went by, we had more people join us and the

quizzes got more silly and more fun too. It wasn't the same as going out but I actually started enjoying these "girls nights in", plus we didn't have the travel time and the drinks were cheaper.

I arranged my first supermarket run in weeks, getting my car out of the garage, it took a while to get started but off I went. I wore my face mask in the store but I was one of the few to be doing so. We all had to queue outside, socially distanced of course, while a member of staff made sure there weren't too many people inside the store. Then another staff member passed a trolley to you, after wiping the handle with disinfectant and we went in, one by one.

It was a surreal experience. The supermarket was nearly empty, we had to follow the markers on the floor and no one wanted to stop too long in case someone else came along behind them. I was very annoyed to find that the plain flour had sold out. How was I going to make shortcrust pastry without flour? When I got home, I wiped down all the shopping I had bought with disinfectant before putting it away. This took longer than the shopping had but I thought it was worthwhile if it helped stop this bloody virus from spreading.

I tried to engage John in conversation about my experience of shopping but he almost shouted to me, "Do you think I haven't got more important things to do than talk about shopping, woman?"

He was trying to help all his clients work out how to use the Government furlough system effectively, so he was under more pressure than ever. It still didn't give the right to talk to me like that but once more, I gave him the benefit of the doubt and decided not to mention it again.

At the start of the Easter Holidays we were all urged to "stay at home" to help protect the NHS. The weather continued to be lovely and one day when doing my daily exercise, and enjoying a walk along the sea front to Holcombe, I spotted Suze on the beach.

She had obviously just been in for a swim and was getting changed. Her house in Dawlish was not far away and she had probably cycled down there as one of her "local" beaches. We stood about 10 yards apart and had a conversation.

"How was the water?" I asked.

"It was lovely, you should try it," she replied.

The sun was out and the sea was looking quite azure. It did look tempting. I decided to take my sandals off and go for a paddle. Suze tried to persuade me to go for a dip in my bra and knickers but I wasn't confident enough for that, plus I hadn't brought a towel.

I tentatively walked into the sea and it was blooming freezing. Suze had followed me at a discrete distance. "You have to be bloody kidding!" I declared to her.

"Don't worry, you get used to it." she replied.

I wasn't so sure but walked in a bit further. I was wearing a short skirt so I was able to wade in just above my knees and bit by bit I got used to the water temperature. After a few minutes I walked back to Suze.

"I have been missing our pool swims." I said. Swimming pools had been closed since the start of lockdown, so our weekly group swims had obviously come to an end. Those swims were good for me in so many ways, a great bit of company and chatting, good aerobic exercise and they got me out of the house.

When that ended with lockdown, I had my daily walks but no company to enjoy it with, plus I would never push myself a bit more with walking like I did with my swimming.

"Come back tomorrow with your swimming gear then." said

Suze "We will have a nice swim. Do you have a hat?"

"Yes. Somewhere."

"Great. Let's come back at 11am tomorrow and we will enjoy a swim. Socially distanced of course!" she winked at me as she said this.

I went home with a purpose, for the first time in weeks I had something to look forward to other than gardening and house maintenance. Though of course there was the trepidation, I didn't think I had swum in the sea in April in Britain since I was a teenager with my family.

The next day was another lovely sunny day. The weather either seemed to be playing with us or supporting us through these troubling times. I was so lucky living so close to Teignmouth and Holcombe Beach, there was nothing to stop me from walking down there for a swim.

I packed my bag, Suze had told me via WhatsApp to bring a warm drink for afterwards, even though the air temperature was warm. Apparently the sea temperature in April is quite cold but fortunately on a day like today, we should warm up quickly afterwards.

On reaching Holcombe, I could see there were a few others swimming or getting ready to swim too. However the tide was out enough to make for a very long beach and therefore none of us would be too close to each other or made to feel awkward by the proximity of others. I walked down the slipway from the Teignmouth end and spotted Suze already there. She was wearing a one-piece swimsuit, a brightly coloured hat and goggles on top of her head.

I set down my gear on the steps a couple of yards away from her and started to get ready. I was wearing my swimsuit under my clothes, so it didn't take long. I was also wearing a one piece swimsuit and hat but no goggles.

“You might want to get goggles if you are going to get your head in the water,” said Suze.

“Oh, I've got them somewhere, I normally wear them to stop my contact lenses coming out,” I replied, “Though I'm not sure if I will get my head in today!”

For some reason my anxiety was rising as we walked towards the sea. It all looked so benign, the waves were light, the sun was shining but I knew how cold it had felt the day before. We reached the waterside and once more I literally got cold feet.

A shiver went down my back but I had to keep going to keep up with Suze who was ploughing through the shallows with purpose. A little wave drove the water up to my thighs and I gave a little yelp but I carried on. Goose pimples started to cover my arms.

Suze carried on walking and then suddenly pushed forward and dived into the water. I reached a level where the water was just above my waist and came to a halt. The next step seemed to be one of the hardest I had ever taken. I built myself up to follow Suze and dive forward.

“Here we go, here we go, let's dive in,” I thought to myself but nothing happened, I was still standing there.

“Come on girl,” I thought again to myself. “You can do this.” The sun was shining down but there was also a light breeze. The goose pimples rose even higher on my arms. Still I stood there. Suze had done a little circuit and was swimming back to me.

“Are you okay, Olivia?” she asked

“Yes I’m fine, just struggling to do that final step.”

“Don't worry, take your time. Why don't you try bobbing down instead of diving in?”

She showed me what she meant. I braced myself, got ready and this time I did it and then...

"Fucking hell it's freezing!" I screamed. Fortunately there was no-one else around to hear my exclamation.

Once in though, it slowly got better. Although I could feel mild pins and needles on my arms and coldness around my waist and chest but not actual pain. I still couldn't get my head in the water though, that was a step too far. I enjoyed the swim but in a way it did seem to go on forever. Eventually Suze said "That's enough, we don't want you getting too cold."

"Thank god," I thought.

I had no idea how long we had been in the water but I could feel bits of me starting to go a little numb. It later turned out we had only been in there 9 minutes and at least a minute or two of that, I had been standing up to my waist. However, it was a start.

As we walked back towards the clothes, I could feel the sun on my back, which was very welcoming.

When we got back we both pulled out our towels and started drying ourselves off.

"Have some of your hot drink," Suze advised. So I leant down to my bag and took out the flask but realised my hands were shaking as I tried to take the lid off and unscrew the cap. In fact my whole body was shivering but when I finally got some of the tea into me it was an amazing feeling. I was still cold but the warmth was beginning to come back.

"Don't take too long getting dry and dressed, otherwise you might get the cold aftershock. Though you should be okay on a warm day like today." Suze added. She looked around her and up to the walkway by the railway, then dropped her towel and quickly whipped on her bra and knickers.

I didn't have her bravery or her finely toned body, so I struggled to get dry with my insufficient towel. I managed to get my knickers on but the bra took forever under the towel. “It’s much easier if you do it without the towel,” Suze laughed.

“But what if someone comes along?”

“Then they might get a cheap thrill!” She laughed again.

This time I placed the towel down, re-adjusted my bra and pulled on the skirt and t-shirt I had in my bag. A few seconds later a couple walked by in full view on the pathway above us. Suze was still standing in her bra but didn't seem to worry or care. I envied her body confidence.

Being honest, I had a reasonable body for my age, my hips and bum were a bit bigger than I would have liked and there was a slight curve to my belly but nothing too much. I had always been active without being overly athletic. My fair hair made feminine grooming slightly easier than some other ladies and since the start of lockdown I had only shaved my legs once.

Now that I had warmed up there was a definite glow to me, as the blood moved around my body and my cold extremities came back to life once more. My fingers were a little white but nothing too bad.

“So, how was it?” Suze asked.

I thought for a moment and then replied. “I loved it.”

“Are you going to go in again?”

“What, now?”

“No, I mean another day. Maybe tomorrow?”

“Why not?”

“Great. I think you have the bug now, Olivia.” Suze smiled.

We parted without any of the normal hugging or kissing. But who knew what was normal nowadays? People talked about the “new normal” but that seemed to be changing every day. We were all still looking forward to the summer when this blasted virus would be behind us and things could get back to some sort of normality. Though we were still slightly concerned it would come back again in the winter, just like the flu.

The walk up the hill from the beach, actually seemed like a blessing rather than a chore, the blood started to flow even more vigorously around my body and I felt more energised than I had in weeks.

Whatever negativity lay ahead, for today I felt good and walked home with a spring in my step.

CHAPTER FIVE

Suze was right, I had caught the bug for wild swimming. It is funny we called it "wild swimming" when all we were doing was going down to our local beaches but apparently wild swimming was the new phrase for all swimming which was non-pool swimming and lockdown was a real boost for the activity in the UK.

Over the next couple of weeks myself and Suze would swim at Holcombe and Teignmouth once or twice a week. It became very important to me as it provided a bit of light release and exercise but was also my main company with another human being. People you passed in the street did say hello but everyone mainly kept their distance from each other, so it wasn't quite the same. Also John and I were barely talking. He seemed to work long hours, we were sleeping in separate beds and would rarely even eat together nowadays.

As I said, I had caught the bug and each day we went I looked forward to my swimming and missed it on the days we stayed on dry land. The weather was glorious but the sea was quite cold. This was part of the buzz though. The initial shock of the cold followed by the acclimatisation and then the warm sun and glow afterwards were all part of the drug-like response I had to this cold-water swimming.

I soon realised that I was also getting acclimatised to the cold water. The initial shock was lessening. I was now getting my head in under the water and staying in longer each time. I was no longer desperate to get out into the sunshine, even though I did enjoy that bit as well.

We also got to know some of the other women who were swimming on the beaches on a regular basis. Some Suze knew already but others were obviously like me and had taken up cold-water swimming during lockdown, as they had no other opportunity to enjoy the activity otherwise. We still kept our distance from each other though, everyone was still on edge in the company of others, though of course some people would mingle in a way in the supermarkets and other "essential" stores.

I hadn't returned to the supermarket in person because I had managed to get a grocery delivery organised, though I had to wait two weeks for my time slot. However, that was a blessing compared with the rigmarole and worry of the supermarket visit. I was able to get the other things we needed from the local fruit and veg shop, which had also stayed open. It was still too early in the year to benefit from my vegetable garden and I had decided to grow even more things for us to eat than normal. We did already have the spring raspberries, which were ripening nicely in the prolonged sunshine.

It was only Suze and I who went for these forays into the sea, as our friends who might have also come lived too far away. One of Suze's friends who liked to swim was cycling to Dawlish Warren and another would walk down to the beach at Maidencombe, but our other friends were landlocked, with no possibility of being allowed to come to the beach under the current rules.

On other days, when I was not swimming, I would go for walks and Suze would do her running or cycling. We were still allowed only one exercise per day and it had to be "local", though none of us was quite sure what local meant.

Then on the 10th May a new announcement was made. We were no longer told to “stay home”, it was now “stay alert”. Everyone was a bit unsure about what that meant but it soon became clear we could travel a bit further for our exercise and we would be allowed more than one outdoor activity a day. This meant that a few others, such as Bren and Suze's friend Dannii could join us on our swims.

Officially, you could only meet one other person from another household for your outdoor activity but we just made sure that none of us got too close to each other, so that although we were there as a group of four or five, we never actually were!

There was a certain irony that this was a time when I really enjoyed the activity and company I shared but it was always underpinned by a big fear and horror of what was going on in the world.

We still kept up the watching of the daily reports on the news. China seemed to be past the worst of the outbreak but countries like the UK, Spain, Italy and US seemed to still be right in the middle of the pandemic.

At first our swimming was restricted to Teignmouth and Holcombe but then Dannii asked if we wanted to go to Maidencombe and that beach was added to our repertoire. I found that it was a lovely little cove with steps down to the beach. There was a deserted cafe on the way down but I think it had been closed since long before Covid.

There were quite a few regular swimmers there, most of whom seemed to know Dannii already and greeted her warmly but a couple of people didn't seem to like her bringing others with her, so they didn't chat to us! Well, stuff them, this was not a private beach and we had as much right as they did to be here. You could argue that some of them had even less rights, as they were not locals but people who had moved recently to the area but I didn't want to go down that street!

The small cove at Maidencombe was a delightful change after the wide open beaches at Teignmouth and Holcombe. I liked both of them but Maidencombe felt a bit more personal and intimate. Suze and Dannii swam out beyond the 5 knot marker buoys and towards one of the other coves but myself and Bren swam out to one buoy and then across to the other before returning back towards the beach. That was more than enough for me and something I wouldn't have dreamed of doing a month or so earlier.

The water was warming up pretty much daily and although the outside weather conditions could be changeable, largely it had been an excellent late spring in the UK, so we were benefiting from some great weather. So we stayed in longer than I had ever done.

Looking back at the coastline from the marker buoy, you could almost sense what most of the coastline of South Devon would have been like before the advent of man to destroy much of it. The cliffs were pure red, punctuated with strips and blobs of green where the plants had got a foothold into the weaker parts of the rocks. The only marks of man were the steep steps leading down to the beach and the redundant and sad looking cafe they passed on their journey.

Just at that moment a cormorant had surfaced close to me. It took one look around before diving once more. I looked across to Bren and indicated where the cormorant had dived and she laughed and nodded. In that moment, I almost forgot all my woes and ducked my head under the water.

Suze had encouraged me over and over again to get my head and face into the water on a regular basis and slowly I had come to re-learn the swimming strokes I had practised as a young girl. Even the three stroke front crawl. Stroke, stroke, stroke and breathe on the right. Stroke stroke, stroke and breathe on the left side. It took time but now I could do it again, though not for too long without puffing a bit. I was not a naturally strong swimmer but I was fairly fit and capable of holding my own with people like Bren and the others.

We meandered slowly back to the beach and got out in the warm sunshine. After a little while Suze and Dannii returned and we all stayed on the beach, basking in the sun, eating and enjoying the picnic we had each brought with us. Everyone kept their own food and drink to themselves and we all still sat apart but it felt a little like normal times.

I was pleased that we had come somewhere different. It had been a lovely day and made me feel happier than I had for some time. I was looking forward to more days like this and possibly investigating more beaches in the days and weeks to come, while we couldn't work.

Not everyone was having the pleasant swim experiences we were though. Some of the beaches at places like Perranporth in Cornwall and Saunton Sands in North Devon got overwhelmed with visitors breaking the restrictions and travelling down from up country to enjoy the sunshine on the beach.

Locals complained that the visitors were parking all over the lanes and blocking routes and eventually the police arrived and started ticketing cars for illegal parking. None of the toilet facilities or cafes were open, so people were going without food and drink and searching for places to relieve themselves. Again locals complained, this time about people peeing in their hedges.

In a way it was a light relief from the more horrific things going on in the world. Devon was still largely immune to these ills but it soon came home to hit us.

We hadn't been seeing much of Jillian as she had not been joining our little swim jaunts and then she had managed to contract Covid from her husband and she was very ill. We were all very worried about her as it was the first person we knew well who had contracted Covid. We heard nothing for a few days but then she contacted us to say that although she and her husband had been very ill, they were starting to feel a little better. The next day, she then let us know that her Mother, who lived in a granny annex next to them, had also caught it and within ten days she was dead. We were all horrified.

Jacqui was only sixty nine years old, really active and in fine health. All the talk in the press and social media was of elderly people or those with "underlying health conditions" as being the ones at risk of dying of Covid. What a load of rubbish, if someone like Jacqui could die, then we were all at risk. It really brought home the reality of this pandemic and made us even more wary. We had been largely protected in this part of rural Devon while people were dying in the towns and cities. Now a lady who was well known to us had died.

John said that there was "probably something wrong with her that we didn't know". But even if there was, we could all be just the same and if Covid had not come along, then Jacqui would still be with us.

What made it even worse was that none of us were able to go to the funeral to support Jillian. The Zoom calls we had with her barely enabled us to console her properly. This was the beginning of Jillian's isolation from our little network. As she was not interested in swimming with us, we would not see her in person and the death of her Mother brought her closer to her sister and cousins, meaning she spent more time with them after that.

Covid had come into our small little network for the first time, bringing death and change and yet, some people locally were still not treating it seriously.

Suze had visited her local shop wearing a mask and had to tell a man without a mask not to get too close to her. He turned around and told her to "Stay at home if you are that fucking worried". He didn't realise who he was dealing with though and Suze tore him to shreds verbally, making multiple references to his ugly face, bad body odour, small brain and the fact that he obviously possessed an even smaller penis. The other shoppers didn't know whether to run away or laugh or both. Suze just finished her shopping and left him in a daze.

CHAPTER SIX

One morning I experienced one of the joys of regular beach swimming. I pulled a pair of clean socks from my sock drawer. I took the first sock and pulled it over my foot but as soon as I did, I felt discomfort and quickly took the sock off.

As I pulled it from my foot, a light spray of something poured over my other bare foot. Slightly confused, I looked at the now inside-out sock but there was nothing on it. I took the other sock and turned it inside out and watched a spray of sand go all over the carpet to join the other sand I had already spread.

I realised what had happened. On the beach one day I must have pulled the socks over my feet while still having sand on them. Somehow this sand had survived me taking the socks off later that day and also a journey through the washing machine, to wait until I went to wear the socks again.

I went and got the vacuum to clear up the mess and went to my socks and tried a few more of them, this time over the sink in the bathroom. It wasn't the only pair to contain sand. After that day I tried to remember to turn the socks inside out before putting them in the washing basket but I didn't always manage it. It wasn't the last time I would spread sand over the bedroom floor.

The other thing that happened sometimes was when I got back to the house after a swim and I went to have a bath or shower. When I took the socks off, the sand that was gathered inside, after the swim, would fly free and go all over the bathroom. Or after my bath or shower, there would be a residue of sand lying there around the plughole, taunting me to clear it away. A small price to pay for the enjoyment I was getting from the actual swimming.

May meandered into the start of June and Suze announced that she thought we were ready for a river swim.

"The water will be lovely now and on a sunny day like today it will be even warmer than the sea."

None of us quite believed her but we went with the flow. She said that we were going to head to Hembury Woods where the River Dart created a large pool between two weirs suitable for swimming.

There was also a nice walk to and from the river, so it would make a nice afternoon out. We arrived in four separate cars (as no one was quite ready to share cars and breathing space yet, even if we had been allowed to), once more there was myself, Suze, Dannii and Bren. There was a layby already full of cars, so I pulled into the National Trust car park, having to navigate around the trees and the tree roots to find a suitable spot to park.

Suze and Dannii were already there chatting and Bren arrived shortly after. It was a lovely warm day and so we were all dressed in summer clothes. The walk was enjoyable through the woods but the trees in full leaf did make it a bit dark and there were already a number of dog walkers out and we had to navigate the odd dog poo that some of the more uncaring dog owners had failed to clear up.

After a while we left the main dog walkers pathway and headed down a steep path which meandered downwards. For the first time I spotted the dark river at the base of the valley, it didn't seem that inviting from here but I could also occasionally feel the sunshine peeping through the full canopy.

Suze set a quick pace and soon we had reached the bottom of the

valley and were walking alongside the river. When we reached a particular tree, Suze double backed under one of the branches on the river side and made her way to a narrow sandy/muddy bank with a little gully leading into the river.
To our right was a wide weir where the sun played gently on the frolicking water. To the left the river wandered back upstream as far as I could see, shrouded by more trees.

We got changed on the narrow strip and placed our bags and gear on the tree roots. Suze was first to get ready and started to descend into the river down the sandy bank. “This is a great place to go in,” she said. “Further up there are lots of sharp rocks which make it difficult to get in but here you can get quite a way in on the sandy river bottom.”

On either side she was flanked by glorious rhododendrons, which were in bloom with their large, vibrant pink flowers. They might be quite invasive but they did look good. Suze halted, then swam forward into the river. Dannii was also used to river swimming and soon followed Suze into the river. Although the sun was shining brightly and the air temperature was warm, the river did look quite dark, cold and foreboding, so Bren and I took a little longer getting in.

The first steps into the water were quite shocking and I felt the rise of the water up my thighs, groin, and stomach much more than I had recently in the sea.

“I thought you said it would be warmer than the sea!” I called out to Suze.

“It is once you’re in!” She laughed back.

Slowly, Bren and I got in. The cold on my shoulders and face was even more shocking, but I soon became acclimatised and we both started swimming up river to follow Suze and Dannii.

I had assumed we would just swim around where we were but they seemed to have a purpose in mind.

Dannii called back over her shoulder, “If you swim upriver first, it is a lot easier coming back with the stream.”

Suze joined in, “sometimes it can be a lot harder than this here, especially after heavy rainfall but as it has been so dry recently the river is being nice to us.”

“Though it does mean we won't really get the swoosh on the way back.” called back Dannii again. I wouldn't experience the “swoosh” until my next visit to Hembury Woods.

The swim up was lovely. Dannii and Suze did stretch ahead of us but they stopped just after a narrow bit in the river and before some rocks. Just when we reached the narrow stretch, Bren and I found the going harder and had to do a few strokes of front crawl. By this time, Suze and Dannii had returned.

“Lie on your back and float down-river” Suze instructed.

I did as she said and although I had to check a few times to stop myself crashing into the bank, I could see why she suggested it. The stream and a few strokes every now and then took you gently down the river while the blue sky passed overhead. What was even more delightful was the sun playing through the leaves and the occasional fish jumping out of the water around us. With my head in the water I was immersed in a special natural world and even when I lifted my head clear, all I could hear was the sound of the water and the occasional bird song. It was truly magical and I could see why some people preferred the rivers to the sea.

This was my first really serene swimming experience and I loved it. I really enjoyed swimming in the sea but this opened up a whole new world to me and really did feel like swimming in the wild.

On the return journey downriver, we passed some other swimmers who had arrived after us and were getting in gingerly from one of the beaches further up river than where we had got in. I could now see what Suze had meant about the rocks as they found it hard to keep their footing but were soon in the water and then it didn't matter. They said hello, as we floated past.

Suze and Danni turned back onto their fronts and did some more front-crawl and were soon further down river while Bren and I enjoyed the gentle breast strokes back to our starting point.

I felt really revitalised and loved standing in the warm sunshine but I actually felt cold. I must have stayed in even longer than I thought and my body shivered despite the warmth and sunshine. After a minute or two my body started to warm up but my fingers did not. I looked at them and realised the main part of my hand was slowly turning blue but the tips of the fingers had gone white. Within a few minutes more they had gone numb and I was unable to use my fingers at all.

I had not experienced anything like this since my earliest swims with Suze at Holcombe. Eventually my fingers started to get some life back into them. But it had taken the lending of a warm cup in my hands to help get the blood flow going.

“It is called Raynaud's Disease,” said Dannii. “Lots of swimmers suffer from it but normally in the colder months. I think you must have stayed in longer than normal and the water is still cold, even though it might not feel it on a day like today.” She let me keep hold of the metal cup and used another one for herself. “The metal is really good when you have got cold hands, it helps with the circulation. You might have to keep an eye on how long you stay in the water.”

“I think you are right. How bloody annoying.” I said. I had found this lovely thing but I couldn't enjoy it for too long because my fingers started to hurt.

“Is there any way of preventing it?” I asked

“You can wear gloves, which works for some people but not all of them," replied Dannii.

"Aren't you supposed to pee on your hands?" Laughed Suze.

"I think you're thinking about jellyfish stings," said Bren.

"No, I know that's an urban myth about jellyfish stings." said Dannii.

"Anyway, I am not gonna start peeing on myself in front of everybody on the beach!" I exclaimed and everyone laughed.

Bit by bit my hands came back to life and we sat and chatted on the river bank.

"Well?" asked Suze.

"Well what?" I answered.

"Well, what did you think of your first river swim?"

"Majestic!" I replied. "But I might wear gloves next time."

Nothing more needed to be said.

CHAPTER SEVEN

24th May 1921 - Lemoncombe Beach

The next day, the same beach. Bert was back again. Something drew him back. It was almost as if he was waiting for something but what it was, he didn't know.

He just sat alone on the beach waiting for something to happen.

He had not alway been alone. He and his wife Doris had enjoyed a fruitful life together before the war. They had regularly enjoyed the delights of the Edwardian society in Torquay and Newton Abbot. After the death of Queen Victoria, the upper middle classes had followed the lead of their King in deciding to enjoy life.

Balls and dances were common place in those days. The young and old all danced, though the older ones looked down on the younger ones who seemed to be dancing with much more gay abandon than they ever had in their day.

The highlights of the social scenes were the horse racing at Newton Abbot and the various regattas along the coast. Bert and Doris both enjoyed the horse racing, plus Bert had been a keen rower and would often take part in the rowing regattas at Torquay and beyond. Doris would always join him and would always help out making afternoon teas.

Bert and Doris were well known in local society, they dined with many families and that even included a young Agatha Miller who would later evolve into the famous writer Agatha Christie.

In fact Agatha's older sister Madge and Doris were very good friends and would often spend time together.

Everyone thought that the life they enjoyed would continue for ever. Britain was at the heart of a global empire, the British were leaders in science, industry and the arts. The young middle classes were more intelligent, prosperous and healthy than any generation before them. This Edwardian era was truly a Golden Age for Britian, what could destroy it?

In 1914 the World changed and those Halcyon days were over. Millions would die during the war and soon afterwards. This included many of Bert's close family and, most hard-hitting to Bert, the death of his dear wife Doris. Hence he was alone while he sat on the beach just a few hundred yards from his home.

Every now and then he would walk back up the steps and lane to his house for a cup of tea, to pay a visit to the toilet or for lunch. But otherwise he was set here for the day.

At around 11am two of his neighbours came down to the beach to walk their dog briefly. He nodded at them and they looked back at him sadly.

Poor Bert they thought. *To have his wife taken away from him when they were both still young.*

The irony that so many people had lost family members and friends in the last seven years was momentarily lost on them as they considered this one man sitting alone on the beach.

Of course Bert was in a better position than the vast majority of those who were also recently widowed. He was very healthy and fit for a man of forty five. He was also rather well off, with a nice house and a passive income that meant he did not need to spend all of his day working.

However, his life was hollow. He had no family, both of his parents were now dead and he had no children. He himself had not been an only child but his two younger brothers had died at Verdun and the Dardanelles. Bert himself had survived the horrors of war, only to return and lose Doris a year later to the Spanish Flu.

The bitter irony was not lost on him.

So now he sat alone, pitied by his neighbours,waiting for something to come but he knew not what.

Another day passed without him learning what that something was.

CHAPTER EIGHT

June 2020 – Haldon Hill

At the beginning of June, the rains finally came again after the long dry spell. My daily forays into the outside world came to an end, which depressed me once more. I didn't even have the pleasure of going into the garden.

When I was able to walk around the Teignmouth area or go for a swim with the girls, I could quickly forget my lack of work and money. Of course there should have been John to support me but he wasn't supportive at all. I heard of other couples who were falling out with each other because they were living in such close proximity to each other for so long, but I seemed to see less of him than I did normally. His life seemed to revolve around work and whenever I tried to engage him, he became short with me and went out to his office in the summer house.

Fortunately, the rainy days didn't last forever but it still made me a little stir-crazy. We were now arranging to swim twice a week. One in a river and one at a beach. I loved the beach swims but the river swims were even better.

We swam at Staverton Halt, which was along an old steam railway where the River Dart stretched in a long gentle pool. It was so still and you could actually swim quite a long way, right up to the old stone road bridge over the River Dart but we didn't get that far. For our sea swims we kept returning to the same few beaches. In theory, although things were opening up again, we were still restricted on how far we could travel.

The next River swim after Staverton was a new one for all of us except Suze. We headed to Salmon Leaps on the River Teign below Castle Drogo. Apparently there were three or four ways to get there but the easiest two were to follow the river. Either downriver from the Whiddon Down road or to walk up river from Fingle Bridge.

We did the latter as we were mainly coming from that side of Dartmoor. We went in two cars (though we all wore masks in the car) and parked up on a muddy roadside. The walk was not all flat, some bits headed up and down some very steep and rocky pathways, so that our legs got a good workout before we had even reached the swim spot. We met others on the walk too, some were ramblers and others were dog walkers but we didn't spot any other swimmers.

The day was cloudy so we didn't have the warm sunshine we had when heading to Hembury Woods, and it felt darker and more sombre. The stretch of water that was our destination was also much smaller than the two previous river swims we had done so I was not sure whether we had actually got there or not when Suze left the path and descended onto a flatter area next to the river.

Up-river we could see a foot bridge passing over the River Teign. Just below us was a series of turbulent pools in which the water moved around in violent maelstroms almost like the insides of a washing machine at full spin.

I was pleased to see we were not going in there, but instead headed to a grassy bank near a jetty to get changed.

"Is that for diving?" asked Bren.

"Only if you want to crack your head open," replied Suze and Bren looked shocked.

Suze continued, "you'll see when you get in."

We all got changed. I was still not quite used to river swims and had brought my new *Rash* vest which had recently arrived by courier, as well as my gloves I wore when river swimming. Bren was also wearing a *Rash* vest but Suze and Danni were just wearing swimming costumes.

The vest and gloves did take a little of the shock from the initial dip into the water but my feet still felt the cold and I vowed to get some boots too.

The swim was actually lovely and the sun eventually started to peep through the clouds. We slowly swam up river but at one point Suze suddenly stood up on a hidden boulder, the water only just coming up to her ankles.

"And that's why you don't dive in along here!" She exclaimed.

There were a few other boulders on the way up to the bridge and I managed to graze my leg on one of them. The current got slightly stronger just as we were coming under the foot-bridge itself and then the water level got too low to swim so we sat in the shallows for a while.

The dog walkers and ramblers continued to pass us.

"Is it cold?" They would ask, or exclaim,"Aren't you brave!"

We tried not to get annoyed by the repetitive and obvious line of questions.

Once more, we swam up-river first so that we were able to enjoy the more leisurely swim back. I did try swimming on my back again but was worried about accidentally swimming into one of the hidden boulders, so I reverted to breaststroke.

Just as I did, a flash of azure blue whizzed past my head.

"Did you see that?" Cried Bren.

"A kingfisher!" replied Suze.

“Oh it was lovely!” I said. “I haven't seen one for years.”

The sun continued to peep through the clouds and the location felt more warm and welcoming all of sudden.

Suze was ahead of the rest of us and had reached the end of the pool. There was a wall with a gap at one end to allow the river water to gush down into one of the square man-made pools.

“These are the jacuzzis, who fancies a whirlpool bath?” She looked around at us but got no agreement or encouragement.

Just as we were all arriving next to her, she slipped along the wall and let herself be taken down into the jacuzzi below.

Immediately, she was washed under the water in the whirlpool of water and I waited for her to re-surface. She didn't do so immediately and when she did, she gasped for air and was pulled under again. We all looked on with worry. Suze was the strongest swimmer out of all of us and there didn't seem much we could do.

Once more she appeared gasping and once more she suddenly disappeared again. I looked around to try and see how we could get down to her to help. Dannii was doing the same, heading to the right of the section where the river flowed into the jacuzzi. The stream was very strong and she had to walk very carefully so as not to get pulled in too.

I went the other way and looked to see if I could get over the wall and climb down without getting pulled into the water.

However, just as I was working out how to clamber down, Suze appeared beneath me coughing and spluttering. She stood with one hand holding the wall and seemed to be able to stand without being buffeted about and dragged under the water.

After a minute of coughing and wheezing she shouted out, “Shit, that was too scary! What a fucking idiot I am!”

Bren asked the stupid question that was probably on all of our lips, “are you okay?”

Suze didn't bother to answer, saying instead, “That was a lot more powerful over there,” she waved back towards where she had gone into the pool. “than I expected. Here,” this time she pointed towards her feet, “is fine though. You have to hold on but it is actually just like a jacuzzi. Come on in.”

“Are you crazy?” said Dannii.

“No it's fine here. Look,” she let go of the wall on the side and was able to stand there at the edge of the pool, where the water descended to the next pool, without holding on.

We were still not convinced but eventually after Suze had recovered her full voice and energy, Dannii asked “But how would we get in? You nearly drowned getting in that way.”

“It was fucking scary,” said Suze. Bren winced at the language - she never did like Suze using certain words.

Suze didn't notice and continued, “if you swing your legs over where Olivia is, you can gently let yourself down and there are some footholds here.”

Dannii seemed the next bravest and did exactly what Suze said. Dannii had a full figure and lowered herself down into Suze's arms. They stayed there for a moment more than they needed to. They weren't a couple and had never been but there was obviously still some physical attraction between the two of them.

Dannii milled about and whooped with enjoyment. Suze explained to her how to stay safe and not get too near the maelstrom. Suze then looked at me expectantly.

Eventually I decided to do what she said. The way down from the wall was further than I thought and the last few inches I had to drop without knowing how deep the water was but I found the floor almost straight away. I momentarily lost my balance and swayed toward the wall and where the water was flowing over it to the next pool but soon regained my upright position.

Once I was in, it was lovely, the fast flowing water flowed around my lower body and you could also sit under the waterfall and enjoy it just like in a jacuzzi. Then I sat below the water flowing over the wall and enjoyed a lovely back massage. I didn't stray too far towards the dangerous end, just bobbed about and even got my head under the water and it was delightful.

Bren could not be persuaded to come in and in fact she started to get out to go and get changed. I realised I had been in longer than I expected, so was thinking of getting out too. Suze started talking to some male walkers on the footpath and Dannii had taken my place underneath the waterfall, letting her shoulders get a massage.

Just then she decided to stand up once more but the water flow had pushed down her swimming costume to display her ample breasts to the two male walkers that Suze was talking to. They were probably both in their early sixties and both looked flustered and shocked.

Suze laughed and said, "put them away you daft besom!"

Dannii also laughed quickly pulling up her costume once more to cover her dignity and spoke to the two men. "Sorry about that gentleman, the water was stronger than I thought. I hope I didn't upset you!"

The look on their faces supported their protestations of "No, not to worry, these things happen," to openly declare that in reality they had loved every second of it and actually these types of things did not happen to them very often.

Suze leaned over and said in a voice that only we could hear, "you tart Dannii!" and proceeded to clamber out of the pool. She waited at the top to help Dannii and myself get out of the pool too before she headed back towards the bank.

The two walkers, having now had their floor show, waved their goodbyes and headed back along the pathway with a few backward glances from time to time.

Suze was shaking her head at Dannii, who just laughed.

"You're only sorry it wasn't you that did that."

"My tits aren't as big as yours though!"

"That's why you show them that tight little bum of yours." Replied Dannii.

Bren was looking even more shocked at the turn the conversation had taken but I knew these two well enough. Plus I had always known Suze to be slightly liberal with her nudity before, and not just around the ladies.

We carried on getting changed while Suze, Dannii and Bren bickered with each other. Either the water was getting warmer or I was getting more used to it, because my fingers didn't feel quite as cold this time. They still went a little numb some twenty minutes later but not as painfully as before.

Perhaps I was now becoming a seasoned wild river swimmer.

Later that evening I knew I was a fully fledged wild swimmer when I bent over to get some salad leaves from the bottom of the fridge and water streamed out of my nose and into the bag!

At first I was horrified, but I soon saw the funny side. It was made even worse when I snorted with laughter and some went back up my nose. I hadn't realised there was any water up there and how come it hadn't just dripped out earlier?

Did this happen to everyone, or was it just me? I made a mental note to ask the girls the next time I saw them.

CHAPTER NINE

On the 15th June some more shops opened up and some people started going back to their offices, including John. But my business was still not able to operate again, so I was stuck in limbo, not knowing what to do.

Legally, people still didn't have to wear masks in shops but a lot of the small retailers were making it mandatory for their customers and staff. We also started getting used to having hand gel by the doorway of a shop and doing the quick hand cleanse as we entered. Some people complained about this but let's be honest, it was a small price to pay for keeping everyone safe.

The pandemic wasn't over but the case numbers seemed to be coming down and as long as we were sensible and thought about things in advance before acting, there seemed to be a feeling that we were getting back to some sort of normality. I was just waiting for when I would be able to welcome back my customers. It was beginning to get frustrating when others could work and I couldn't, plus I knew some people were breaking the rules and carrying on.

I couldn't do that though.

A week later the news got even better, for the first time in months there were less than 1000 new cases in the UK. Were we getting towards the end of this bloody pandemic? Was the light beginning to appear at the end of the tunnel?

We had to hope so...

A few days later, the weather got even better and suddenly it was hot, really hot!

Swimming here we come!

But then the news was full of people swarming to beaches like Bournemouth in their thousands. It was a bit like the Saunton Sands experience in the first lockdown but even worse.

Our little group of ladies was wary about going anywhere too busy and also about being classed just like those stupid people all swarming to the same beaches. But perhaps they weren't so stupid. Perhaps they were just ordinary people who had been confined to their flats or houses with nowhere to go. I'd been lucky to be able to enjoy so much of the Devon countryside, it was easy to judge others who weren't so lucky.

The main thing that worried us was the chance that Covid would spread more widely down our way now, as we seemed to have bypassed it largely so far, except from a few notable examples like Jillian's Mum.

Worryingly Jilian herself was still struggling with the after-effects of Covid. She seemed to have a continual cough and struggled to speak sometimes. She also seemed overly tired. At the time we didn't know what was wrong with her but later we would come to know that this was "Long Covid".

In the meantime Dannii announced that we were heading somewhere different this time for our swim. We were going to go in one car but get away from the crowds. We were heading up onto Dartmoor to go to Crazywell Pool.

Crazywell was one of those old quarries which had lots of ancient myths surrounding it. It had been one of those hidden gems until it had been included in a popular swim/walk book, so now more people were finding out about it. However, while the weather was good and the beaches were manically busy, it was a good location to head towards.

Dannii explained that there were three or four different ways to get there but because we didn't have masses of time, we decided to go to Princetown and then parked up near the old tin mining Whiteworks.

From there it was about a thirty to forty minute walk across some open moorland, which was part of the experience. This wasn't somewhere for all the family or the more sedentary swimmers.

It was the regular four of us - Dannii, Bren, Suze and myself -crammed into Dannii's battered old VW beetle, all wearing masks of course. The journey was an experience in itself. We headed up onto the moor from the Ashburton turn off the A38 and crossed the Dart for the first time at New Bridge. We laughed at the masses of cars already there for kayakers, walkers and swimmers heading to Spitchwick or maybe even to Sharrah Pool. We hoped our destination would not be anywhere as busy as this!

I wasn't sure if Dannii's car was going to make it up the hill after New Bridge, but with a bit of jostling and rocking in our seats from the four of us, she managed it. I also felt sorry for the occupants of the car that followed us, who received a blast of petrol smoke at every gear change.

We kept going through Poundsgate, Dartmeet, Two Bridges and Princetown before finally arriving at a dead end lane heading towards Whiteworks. It was a single lane and we did have to wait for one car heading in the opposite direction, as well as a flock of sheep who didn't want to get out of the way until Dannii beeped her horn and swore out of the window, “get out of the fuckin' way you fuckin' sheep”.

Soon after, we parked up and started our way across the open moor. This was more like it. It reminded me of my childhood, rambling across the rugged parts of Dartmoor with my parents. Dannii led the way this time, cutting across wider pathways before dropping into a valley and crossing a shallow stream.

Ahead I could see a large stretch of water. “Is that Crazywell?” I asked.

Dannii laughed, “no that is soddin' Burrator reservoir!”

When I was able to get my perspective right, I could see it was probably bigger than a pool. But from the other point of view, I had no idea how big this pool was.

We carried on along a rugged but clearly defined path, until Dannii took us on a small diversion towards a large stone cross where we stopped to take a few photos with the cross and the reservoir behind us. Recording our swims with photos and the experiences around the swim was becoming the norm and a key factor in this swim logging, was the growing number of swim Facebook groups that were popping up. This was more Dannii's realm but I had started following a few threads to learn more, plus I knew our photos would be on Facebook later that day.

After this short diversion, we returned to the large path once more. It looked like we were heading straight for the reservoir but suddenly Dannii turned, leading us up a slope. Once more we passed a stone cross, so I asked “are we just here for more photos?”

“No, the pool is just over there.” She pointed ahead but I couldn't make anything out. Surprisingly though, I could make out cars driving in the distance. When I pointed this out it was Suze that replied. “That’s the Yelverton to Princetown road. It is further away than you think.”

We carried on walking and suddenly in front of us was a large pool - much larger than I was expecting. We descended a gravelly path to a lovely sheltered little grassy dell, where you could walk straight into the pool.

We laid out our things and started to get changed. Both Dannii and Suze stripped off but didn't get their cossies on.

“So, are we skinny dipping then?” Asked Danni.

Bren looked aghast. “What if someone comes?”

“So what?” Replied Dannii. “There is no-one for miles and even if someone does come, no-one cares.”

Just at that moment, a family came up the hill from the Burrator direction. Suze and Dannii picked up their towels and their swimming costumes. Bren gave them both a superior look.

I put my cossie on and followed the others into the pool. After the warmth of the sun, the water was much, much colder than I was expecting but it was surprising how quickly I became acclimatised to the temperature and soon I was frolicking around with the others.

We must have stayed in for a good fifteen minutes before getting out and the warm sun that greeted us was lovely. The family was long gone and no one else came to replace them, so Suze and Dannii took off their swimming costumes, spread their towels out and languished in the sun, taking no notice of their nudity. Whereas after taking my cossie off, I wrapped my towel around me despite the warm sun, just in case someone came along. Though when I got changed I didn't worry too much about keeping covered up when putting on my knickers and bra.

Bren was her normal restrained self, carefully keeping herself covered up while getting changed, while Dannii and Suze continued to bask in the sunshine naked.

Eventually they got up and got some of their clothes on, but were interrupted by a sudden loud noise from the top right corner of the bank around the pool. As we all looked up, there appeared about two dozen squaddies on a march. Suze and Dannii could not help laughing.

“Perhaps we should strip off again?” Dannii joked.

“What, doing a service for our servicemen you mean?” replied Suze and they laughed again.

The squaddies carried on down the slope and away, not realising how close they had been to some female delights but also some feminine danger!

CHAPTER TEN

We had enjoyed a few days of lovely weather and some great swims. We were still in the middle of a pandemic but for us life was as good as it could be in such tragic circumstances. I had a good home, a reasonable partner who was still able to work, even if I couldn't. Plus I had some great friends and the opportunity to enjoy the amazing Devon countryside.

But then my world collapsed in a way I couldn't have imagined.

It all happened very suddenly. I came home after a lovely walk in the nearby woods, feeling very positive about life in general and John greeted me with a stern look and said he wanted to chat about something. That was the understatement of the year.

He announced that he was leaving me to live with another woman who was pregnant by him. Every part of my body crashed to the floor when he told me, I just couldn't comprehend what was happening. What made it even worse was that “The Woman” (that was how she later became referred to by me) was older than me. Part of me might have understood if he had gone for a younger model, perhaps a young, blonde bimbo called Kylie, but no, he ended up with a middle-aged accountant lady called Beryl for God's sake.

What made it even worse was that John shafted me true and proper. “Our” house was actually his in word and deed. Even though we had jointly been paying the mortgage for the last eighteen years, everything was in his name “for tax purposes” and in reality all I had been doing was paying rent. So, I was asked to leave and give up the home I had helped build and establish.

John even turned our friends against me by telling them some spurious tales about some of my actions. Lying about me having multiple love affairs (even though it was he who got another lady pregnant). About my rages and violent conduct. And so much more. What shocked me most was that they were prepared to believe him. He had apparently been laying the trails for his lies for years, so they readily believed these things about me now.

Therefore, with practically no notice, I left our home and had to find somewhere to live, pretty quickly. The day after he made the announcement, he walked me around the house talking through the things that were his and mine. I was in such a daze I barely knew what was happening and practically acceded to everything he said. In the end it meant that most of the furniture and appliances stayed with John in the house and the few things that "we" decided were mine would be taken with me, when I was ready.

"You can stay in the house for a week while you find somewhere to go." he said, as if he was being kind.

I couldn't stay in the house a moment longer with him though so I called Suze, who said I could come around. I packed up some bits and pieces and drove straight over to her house.

CHAPTER ELEVEN

I had reached a new low. For the first time in over twenty five years, I was homeless. I had been living with John for eighteen years and the seven years before that I had been renting my own home quite happily. Before that I had lived with my parents for a few years after a previous relationship had fallen through.

My small amounts of savings were eaten up with the cost of moving and finding new furniture, white goods, etc and I had no hope of getting a mortgage at this time because of my current lack of work.

This was the hardest time that I could remember. My parents were no longer alive, I had no siblings and nowhere to live. Suze was amazing and put me up while I tried to find a flat but we were still in the heart of the pandemic so it wasn't easy.

Eventually I found an apartment in Teignmouth which was in a great location but it was only a one-bedroom apartment, and it didn't have any parking. I had to do the viewing via Internet video because of the current restrictions and it looked okay so I decided to go for it.

It turned out to be a good decision as the flat was in a great position, close to town and the beach and therefore what I needed right now (although later I would rue the lack of an extra bedroom for doing treatments). What I hadn't counted on was the state of the property. I had forgotten what some rental people thought about the property they were living in and that they had no worries about leaving it in a terrible state for the next tenant.

The landlord hadn't bothered either, whether he would have in normal times, I wasn't sure, but he managed to carefully hide the state of the property during my video viewing.

Some things just needed an ordinary clean with a good vacuum cleaner and for me to get the duster and marigolds out. Some things needed a lot more. The kitchen had congealed fat in places that I couldn't work out how they had managed to get it there. The loo was absolutely disgusting and the shower and bath plugs were blocked up with hair. I didn't want to think too much about what type of hair, though some of it was definitely short and curly.

It was all too much for me. I slumped on to the bathroom floor and wept openly. I could see myself in the stained mirror and that made me cry even more. I was not sure how long I sat there and cried but it was my lowest point for some time.

I had originally arrived with most of my things in my car but decided to ask Suze whether I could stay for a few more days at her place while I cleaned the apartment.

In the end it took me three days and I nearly gave up more than once but I had nothing else to do with my time and nowhere else to go.

By the end of it, I had a lovely but small apartment within walking distance of the beach at Teignmouth and with handy walks nearby. I would also be able to head into town when all the shops opened up again. The only issues were that I had no spare room to do treatments in and also I had to walk a few hundred yards to get to my car. The alternative for which was to pay an exorbitant fee to park my car in one of the car parks nearby and even then I couldn’t use that during the day!

But what really hurt was the loneliness. Even though I had not had much love or affection in recent months from John, he was still at home when I needed company. With so many restrictions on what we could do, there was no-one to take his place. I had never been so alone.

Where I really felt it was the first night in the apartment on my own. I had got the television set up and managed to cook myself a simple tea, which I ate on my lap in front of an old episode of Midsomer Murders. The telly programme was warm and comforting, as I enjoyed the interplay of the detective and his sergeant. But it was still about murder, so that when a really scary bit happened, I automatically went to turn to John but of course, he wasn't there.

This brought it home to me. I had lost my partner, my home and my life. I headed to the bedroom after the programme ended, feeling utterly depressed and alone. I had no one to cuddle, no one to feel warm next to in bed and no one to talk to when I needed it.

Yes, I had my small circle of friends and we had our swims but they were only two or three times a week at most and each time I would head home to an empty apartment to spend the rest of the time on my own.

CHAPTER TWELVE

A few days later we returned to Maidencombe on a slightly overcast day, the weather matching my feelings. This time Dannii's cousin Terry joined us. He was the first man to join us on one of our swims. Of course there were many male swimmers but generally we found there were less men swimming in cold water than women.

There were a number of theories why. Some thought it was down to the counteracting effects of cold water on hot flushes, but that didn't explain the younger and older women who loved cold water swimming.

Another hypothesis was that women were more impervious to pain and therefore less likely to feel the negative effects of the cold water. Though I wasn't sure if this was based on fact or hearsay.

Suze said that women naturally liked to congregate together in groups, which was ideal for popping along to the beach for a chat and a quick swim. Whereas men would do that in sports teams and competition and therefore would tend to do swimming to the extreme, going further and faster. Of course many women were doing triathlons, long distance swimming and other swimming to the extreme but many just wanted to "swimble" which was a new name for a cross between swimming and bimbling!

Dannii had also suggested that men were naturally peacocks who liked to posture and flaunt themselves in front of women.

Of course they could do this on the beach but unfortunately the negative effects of the cold water on some parts of the male anatomy might make their posturing less impressive!

Terry actually wasn't much of a swimmer but obviously thought he looked quite good in shorts on the beach. He was in his mid thirties, had a good tan and curly mop of hair and all he lacked was a medallion. He and I swam out to the buoy and back while Suze and Dannii swam out further.

After the two of us had returned to the beach we shared a few words, as we dried ourselves off. After doing this he covered himself in body oil, caressing his chest as he did so. I tried not to laugh too much.

Soon afterwards, Dannii and Suze returned and I was spared trying to make much more conversation with him.

Imagine my disappointment when a couple of days later at Ness Cove, Dannii failed to turn up and Terry came in her place.

"Where is Dannii?" I asked.

"She couldn't make it and thought we would be better off, just the two of us."

I rolled my eyes. We both got changed. I turned my back as he was looking straight at me. I was very careful to make sure I was covered up at all times, something we didn't always worry too much about when it was just the girls.

When we were both changed he said "Shall we go in then?"

I nodded my assent and we both walked towards the beach. He walked very close to me so that our arms brushed each other from time to time.

"Remember we need to social distance." I said in a jovial voice, as if making a joke and I took a step sideways to distance myself from him.

“Oh, we should be okay outside and neither of us have symptoms.” he replied and stepped closer again.

“I'd rather you didn't though and we have to be careful and protect others, I’m -” I paused for a second and said “I’m seeing my Mum later and she’s at risk, so I have to be careful, sorry.” It was a white lie but I couldn't think of anything else in the moment.

Once more I stepped aside and this time he didn't try to get closer again. I’m not sure what made me lie about my Mother, she had actually died about 5 years earlier but I had to do something and I didn't want to shout out “fuck off” on the beach or even worse, make him aggressive.

We actually had a nice swim and even a bit of a chat. At first I swam away from him but as he made no attempt to get too close to me, I followed him out towards the buoy and back and then we returned to the beach.

“I enjoyed that Olivia, and I enjoyed your company,” he said.

I did feel a bit sorry for him but then I felt he was looking at me all over while he said this.

I just mumbled in return and once more turned my back on him while we got changed.

“Would you like to swim again some time?” He said.

I groaned inwardly. How could I get rid of him?

“Sorry Terry, but I prefer swimming with the girls if that is alright?”

“No worries babe, I can dig that.”

What? 'Babe'. "Dig'. Why had he suddenly turned into a 1970s porn star?

"Thanks. Oh there's Kim, sorry I need to go and say hello." I waved at the fictional Kim up on the steps and headed off before he could say anything else.

I quickly made my way up the steps and back to my car. When I had got back on to the main road, I used the voice control to call Dannii.

"Hello?"

"Where were you today?" I asked.

"Oh I couldn't make it babe," she replied.

That word again!

"You left me with your bloody cousin, it was awful!"

I could hear laughing down the line.

"Oh darling, we knew you needed some cock and we thought Terry would do nicely."

"You have got to be kidding. He thinks he is Magnum PI and would rather look at himself in a mirror than compliment a lady. I'm not really looking for anyone right now and even if I was, it would be an old-fashioned type of man who can respect me and be gentle with me. There doesn't seem to be anyone like that any more."

"Oh babe, we will find you one."

"No thanks, when I do want to look, I'll find someone myself." I hung up.

I headed home on my own, to my empty flat. It was days like this that I felt really alone. Heading home after a lovely day out to an empty, cold flat.

I got changed into my Pjs and put on a crappy film. I was one of those people who either loved great films from the 30s, 40s and 50s like “It's a Wonderful Life” or “Kinds Hearts and Coronets” or “The Ladykillers”. Or I loved rubbishy films from the 1980s like “Flashdance”, “The Breakfast Club” or “Pretty in Pink”. Tonight's choice was the classic “Dirty Dancing”.

I'd find myself reliving every moment that Baby experienced and saying half the lines but I still loved it. I also polished off a box of maltesers and three gin and tonics. This was what my life had become.

I couldn't get to sleep, so I decided to check out one of the online dating sites I had glanced at a few days earlier. But I wasn't in the right mood and couldn't work out how to use it. I wanted to get an idea of the type of people on there but it was asking me a load of crazy questions, so I gave up. I decided I wasn't ready to start dating anyway.

CHAPTER THIRTEEN

26th May 1921 - Torquay, South Devon

Bert wasn't heading to the beach today, he was going to see his attorney, John Tuck, in Torquay.

"You need to take on an estate manager Bert." Tuck was saying. "Someone who can deal with the tenants and the farmers for you. It is not your thing and if you get the right person, it could make a big difference to how successful your business is."

"I know that John but I don't know anyone who would be right. Will you have a look for me?"

"Of course I will. By the way we still have the issue of Mrs Sandford. Her rent is now six months overdue."

"She can't pay me John. Her husband died at the saw mill last year, she has three children all under working age and the last i heard she was holding down two jobs to make ends meet."

" Three" said Tuck.

"What?" asked Bert.

"Three jobs now. She is taking in washing. She cleans the pub. And now she is also looking after two more children for the woman next door."

"Exactly! She is working so hard and yet all the jobs are poorly paid, so she doesn't have enough for my rent as well. I'll go and visit her tomorrow."

The rest of the matters did not take much time but when Bert left Torquay the rain came down heavily. Therefore he decided not to head down to the beach today. For some reason, he felt the need was not so keen today but he must go there tomorrow.

He went home to his lonely house. Yes, he did have Mr and Mrs Holmes but they lived in a little cottage in the village rather than the house. The servants who did live in the house with him, would be up on the top floor in their private rooms.

So Bert sat alone in his drawing room nursing a small whisky and soda. He had no one to talk to, no one to go on walks with and no one to share other experiences with.

He didn't admit it to himself but this seemed to be the driving force in making him visit the beach. Why? He did not know.

CHAPTER FOURTEEN

4th July 2020 - Teignmouth

The 4th of July. The Americans were celebrating overthrowing the British but most of us ladies were celebrating the fact that we could go and get a haircut again.

I must admit I was not a hairdresser junkie like some of my friends, but it was still nice to be pampered. I had let my hair grow longer than normal in the past few months and I did like the new length. However the fringe and the split ends were beginning to get to me.

Of course I didn't organise an appointment for the actual 4th but somehow I had managed to get one with my local hairdresser on the 6th, so there wouldn't be too long to wait.

I still couldn't work but it sounded like that would not be for too much longer, I had a number of people asking about appointments and so I decided to start filling my own diary up in preparation and hope that Boris wouldn't change the rules again.

The haircut and shampoo were lovely, the stylist wore a mask as well as a visor, which kept getting steamed up. But we were all just delighted to be in there once more, so no one seemed to mind.

On the 13th July I performed my first Bowen treatment in over four months. I actually did six treatments that day, driving around from house to house with my massage bed and mask in hand.

It was hard work. I realised I was slightly out of practice and had to think about things which would have come instinctively before. Also I wasn't quite as fit as I thought. Obviously I had been swimming and walking but the treatments took muscles and postures that I hadn't been using for months.

The response from my customers was amazing though, they seemed to feel the same way I felt about their treatment as I did about my haircut. For the first time in weeks, I had something to be positive about. The sun was shining, the schools were soon to break up and I was back at work. Perhaps things were beginning to get back to normal.

Bizarrely, the Government finally announced mandatory face masks in shops. Why they hadn't done that months ago, no one was quite sure, but it did give us more confidence going into shops, though some people still seemed to ignore the regulations.

True to form, when the school holidays started, the rains came but I didn't care for a while as I was back working and that kept me going.

July rolled into August. Infection rates rose in some of the cities and Leicester was placed under special restrictions. Our tellies were full of pictures of people ignoring social distancing in these urban areas and wondering why the rates were shooting up and their local areas were placed under greater restrictions.

At the same time the weather conditions were up and down and most of us were also back at work, so we didn't swim as much as we had in June but we all felt it important to keep going, so we did manage to swim most weeks, mainly in the evenings.

On the busier days in the summer holidays, the beaches were quite busy, so Suze suggested another new swim experience. She suggested going to Maidencombe but swimming around to the next cove.

She and Dannii had done it a number of times but this was a first for me. Bren decided to come to the beach but not swim around to Blackaller's Cove which was the next cove around. We arrived at Maidencombe Beach and it was already busy, so Dannii led us on to the rocks to the right of the steps as it was less busy and we could go into the sea directly from there. We all got changed and Dannii gave me her spare dry bag tow-float, so I could take my phone, keys and a drink with me.

From the rocks the sea did look even more attractive, especially in the lovely sunshine. The water was quite azure and you could spot some small fish swimming over the rocks and sands.

We all got into the water and dodged around the multiple paddle boarders. One of them, according to Dannii, was apparently a famous England and Exeter rugby player. He did have a very fit body covered in tattoos and seemed to be having fun with his kiddies.

The tow-floats not only served as dry protection but also to help us be seen amongst all the various crafts on the sea that day. As we had chosen to arrive at low tide, we were able to walk at chest height for quite a way towards the marker buoy but then had to start swimming.

Suze and Dannii always did a mixture of front crawl and breaststroke but my front crawl was not as good as theirs and I could not keep it up for long, so they quickly pulled ahead of me.

They turned, waited, and then started again. Surprisingly quickly I could see the signs of two beaches around the corner. Perhaps this wasn't going to be as bad as I thought. Suze and Dannii had said that if I did get knackered I could always “rock-hop” back to Maidencombe but I was determined not to need to do that on this occasion.

When we had fully rounded the rocks, the swimming became

slightly harder and once more I started to drift behind Suze and Dannii. They seemed perfectly at ease and happily waited for me. The first cove, called Blackaller's, seemed a bit closer now and the other, called Mackerel Cove, also didn't seem that far away. Perhaps I could make it there, I thought, and I said as much to Dannii and Suze, who just looked at each other without saying anything.

We pressed forward once again but after a few more minutes it seemed like the coves were not getting any closer but when I turned around I could see we had come another 100 yards or so, it must just be the perspective which made it seem like we were making no progress.

"Do you think you can make it to Mackerel Cove?" asked Suze.

Between puffs of breath I replied, "no, maybe not."

Eventually we came level with the first cove but it still took a few more minutes to actually get to the shore. After a bit of wheezing and panting, I was able to stand up again and then make my way up onto the beach proper.

The sun was shining on us and I realised that this was the first time I had ever walked on a beach that you couldn't get to by foot. Suze and Dannii had already opened their dry bags and were both having a drink, whereas I needed a little longer to recover.

After they had lounged and drunk for a bit, Suze and Dannii announced they were heading around to the next cove and so I bade them farewell with my blessing.

Dannii shouted back over her shoulder, "strip off and enjoy your virgin beach!"
She and Suze laughed and were soon disappearing off into the distance.

When I had had a drink, I decided to explore this new beach of mine but quickly realised there was not much to it. Just a small sandy area surrounded by red sandstone rocks and steep cliffs.

I looked around and there was no one in sight, no swimmers, kayakers, paddle boarders (who seemed to have all headed in the other direction) or boats.

Could I strip off?

It was very tempting, the sun was gorgeous and I was there alone like some kind of modern day Robinson Crusoe on my virgin sands.

Eventually I decided to go for it but just at that moment I heard a dull thrumming behind me. I turned, wondering what the noise was and then I spotted it. An orange boat was scything through the water in line with the coast, on board were a number of people holding phones and binoculars and they were all pointing them towards the shore and me.

Even though I had not stripped off I felt exposed by the thoughts of it and I quickly dived into the water and actually swam down under the surface. Eventually, I mustered the courage to look back out to sea and I could see that the boat had long since disappeared around the bay. Soon afterwards I saw Suze and Dannii returning once more, so I decided to swim out and get a head start on them so they could catch me up.

It didn't take them long to catch up, even though they had already swum around from the other cove. We made our way back around the rocks and across Maidencombe to the rocks where we had left our main bags. Bren was there and basking in the sunshine, so we all decided to join her lying on the rocks for a while even though it was not that comfortable.

Dannii and Suze recounted how they had swum around to Mackerel Cove and that it was lovely there. “How did your naturism go Olivia?” asked Dannii with a wicked smile.

Bren turned to look at me quickly. At first I wasn't going to say anything but then I decided, why not? So I told them all about thinking about stripping off but then about the sea safari boat and me diving under the surface.

Bren looked shocked but Dannii and Suze just guffawed with laughter. I had never known anyone actually guffaw before but they did it. So loud were they that everyone nearby turned around to look. Even though they didn't know what had happened, they all looked at me. I vowed not to tell anyone else about it and not to skinny dip again soon!

CHAPTER FIFTEEN

The idea of skinny dipping was definitely the exception rather than the rule, when we did go swimming we would wear our costumes whether there were people around or not. The rest of August was a mixture of work, swimming and life slowly heading towards some kind of normality for me.

Of course the current normality was everyone keeping a distance from each other, wearing masks in public and not shaking hands. Also for me, it meant my new life without John.

As people were able to travel around again, the Westcountry and its beaches got busier and busier. In order to get away from the masses of holiday makers, we tended to steer clear of the busiest beaches in Teignmouth, Dawlish, Torquay and Paignton.

National Trust car parks on the coast and the moors became our primary destinations, followed normally by a one or two mile walk to much quieter beaches or pools than those you could just turn up and swim at.

Maceley Cove, Great Mattiscombe, Leas Foot, Soar Mill Cove, Moor Sands; these beaches took longer to get to but they were worth it. The drives through the country lanes of the South Hams took some time, most especially during the summer holidays, but if you then were willing to walk a bit to get to the beaches, you would be rewarded with beaches which were less busy than others. Plus some of them were the most delightful beaches I had yet visited – a mixture of white sands or pebbles and azure seas, were magnificent.

One day we headed to the National Trust Car Park near Ayrmer Cove. It was a gloriously sunny day and when we walked down to the beach we were slightly disappointed to see around thirty people already there. During the late morning and early afternoon a few dozen more people arrived, so it felt quite busy to us.

While we were there we decided to walk up the steep hill to see along the coast a bit, as we browed the hill we could see down to the static caravans of Challaborough below us but what caught our eye were the people on the beach there and also on Bigbury sands ahead of us and on Bantham beach in the near distance. They looked like masses of ants moving around. Hardly a bit of sand was not covered in people. I looked wistfully towards Burgh Island, I would not be going there today and I was glad, as I watched the numerous people on the small causeway of sand between Bigbury and the Island.

We made our way back down to Ayrmer Cove with some happiness, we had obviously chosen well on this hot sunny day. Our little beach was not so packed after all!

Devon had probably not been this busy since before the Second World War - holiday parks were booming and everyone with a spare room was letting it out for holiday makers. Letting agents stopped letting their flats to locals because they could make even more in the holiday business. A one bed flat which might make £600 pcm for a long term let could suddenly make nearly £3000 in July or August.

I started to get worried about my own little flat. Would I still have a roof over my head?

Work was busy and I was beginning to get my full working capability back. This meant I was no longer feeling tired by the end of the day and we would often go and swim in the evenings. Although we would not readily mix with others, we started to meet more and more “wild swimmers” at different locations and chat about our interests.

Suze decide to arrange a break down in Cornwall for four of us - myself, Dannii, Bren and of course herself. It was planned for the middle of September and we looked forward to the possibility of some swimming when we were down there as apparently some of the beaches were amazing.

CHAPTER SIXTEEN

On the 1st September, the schools opened up again. Everyone waited with baited breath to see whether there would be a new wave of Covid. What was even more concerning was the impending return of students to university. Surely they would be hotbeds of infections of Covid?

Students will be students and the chances of social distancing with Freshers meeting each other for the first time was ludicrous. Plus there would be people coming from all over the UK, mixing and then spreading it around again. Then the news came out that the rates of infection were on the rise and a third of those recent infections were for people aged 20-29.... hmmm, we could only guess what was going to happen.

For the first time since March the 'R rate' of infection had gone back above 1. To counter this, the "rule of six" was brought back, so we couldn't gather in groups of more than six people. A thing that I hadn't actually done since March anyway!

With the 'R rate' still on the rise, the time came for our short break in Cornwall. We had some debate as to whether we should go or not but Suze argued that if we take all our own food and drink and don't integrate with anyone else, we would be fine.

So with some trepidation, the four of us got in a car together for our four day break in West Cornwall. We had a lovely two bedroom cottage in the town of Porthcurno which, somewhat surprisingly, Bren seemed to know rather well.

The journey wasn't quite as bad as I expected. Although

Porthcurno was about as far as you could go in Cornwall, the A30 from Exeter made its way nearly all the way to the town. We were able to stop in Hayle for some provisions at Marks and Sparks before heading down to our destination and arriving at about 4pm.

The apartment was one of many converted from one large building and we had to carry our bags up some very steep steps to get into the apartment but once we were in there, the views from the balcony were outstanding. You could see the wooded hillsides which formed the valley of Porthcurno and led down to dramatic views of the sea.

There were two bedrooms. Suze and Dannii shared the double and Bren and I shared the twin. Although it was September, we seemed to have gotten lucky with the weather and the sun was shining bright and hot.

"Shall we head to the beach then?" Said Dannii.

"Why not?" Said Suze.

So within minutes of arriving we were walking down the road with cossies already on and towels in our hands.

The beach was a majestic cove of white sand heading down to a blue sea and absolutely packed. We had arrived at just after 4:30pm and the sun was just beginning to disappear from the right hand side of the beach, so people were picking up their things and moving towards the other side.

We found a fairly isolated spot on the white sands and took off our outer clothing before walking down the beach to the sea. The beach was fairly flat at first but then descended steeply to the water's edge. The waves were throwing up a fair bit of surf but there were quite a few swimmers in there, so obviously it wasn't too bad. And the water was a gorgeous cerulean blue. With the white sands it made it look like the Caribbean.

It didn't feel like it though. The water was definitely a bit colder than back in Devon but we soon acclimatised to it and had a bob and swim in the water. Bren then suggested a walk around to the next beach as it was low tide.

I thought she meant to go up onto the headland but she meant to stay on the beach and then wade through the shallow water towards the left, so we made our way to the next beach. There were already a few people milling about on the sand and even more people swimming in the shallows. This was idyllic, the water was so clear and shallow over the white sands, you couldn't help but enjoy it. We mucked about more than we would do at home. Bobbing in the waves and diving under each other. It was great fun.

The sun dropped even lower and even though it was still light, the temperature was dropping quickly, so we decided to head back to the main beach before the tide came back in too far.

When we did, we realised that the sun had disappeared from half of the main beach and our bags and clothes were in the shade. We hurried to get our clothes on, and considered going to the sunny side of the beach but it was already packed and we decided to just dry the worst off ourselves and walk back with our light dresses over our damp cossies.

It only took us 10 minutes to get back to the apartment but it was harder on the return as it was all uphill. There then followed the scramble for the two showers. Bren and I agreed on our order but we could hear Suze and Dannii next door arguing about it. I went into the shower after Bren and could feel the sand on the floor of the shower but it was so white that you could barely see it.

We had decided not to go out to eat and everyone agreed to eat vegetarian for the duration of our stay if I would do the cooking. John used to tell me I was an adequate cook rather than a good one but that was partly because he expected me, the woman, to cook his meals for him, even though I had no experience of cooking meals with meat. This was another reason why I now hated him with the benefit of hindsight and with my rose-tinted glasses removed.

The reality was that when I was cooking vegetarian meals, I was much more than an adequate cook but for our first meal, I cheated and just cooked the ready-made dishes we had bought in M&S in Hayle on the way down the A30.

Tonight's culinary experience was Mushroom Wellington with a mixture of vegetable dishes.

We placed the dishes in the middle of the table in the dining area. From here you could see the sea, but only when standing up. However the slowly disappearing sunshine made for a lovely colour in the sky and we enjoyed our meal.

Everyone served themselves from the dishes in the centre and I had made sure that there was more than enough for everybody, so we were able to help ourselves to seconds. Unfortunately it was on her third effort of refilling her plate that Bren had stood up and leaned forward more than she had before. As she bent forward to reach the last bit of truffle oil cauliflower cheese, she must have reached an angle she hadn't managed so far and sea water streamed from her nose onto her plate. We all burst into laughter as the water streamed down and Bren leaped back in anguish dropping her plate in the process. Fortunately she had managed to only stream the water onto her own plate but she was mortified nonetheless.

As we were all seasoned sea swimmers now, we had all experienced the same problem, albeit not normally in company. But Bren was still highly embarrassed to have had it happen to her and onto the food as well. We all told her to get over it, despite silently thinking we had some good ammunition for future mockery.

CHAPTER SEVENTEEN

Despite the incident with the nose water, Bren recovered enough to plan the next day's adventure. Partly because she knew the area well but also because she wanted to head to Penberth because of the Poldark connection. She had then given us the talk about Poldark, where it was filmed and how gorgeous the lead actor was.

When she and her husband had visited the area two years earlier, the car park at Porthcurno was full of television vehicles as they were using it as their main base. She had then made her husband follow her in tracking down filming locations in and around the area, in case they could see some of it happening. They had managed to track down one location but it was only just being set up, so they had to return the next day (to her husband's chagrin) to stand in the mist and drizzle while they watched filming from a hundred yards away. The filming was over now but she still wanted to check out the location of quite a lot of the filming.

We made packed lunches including lots of drinks (because the day was set to be very warm) and headed along the inland route behind the Telegraph Museum towards Treen. From Treen we walked through fields towards Penberth, heading down a steep hill into the valley. The last bit of the walk into Penberth was along the road which belied the destination we were soon to reach.

When we got there it was like stepping back in time to an old fishing cove, with a large cobbled wharf down to the sea and small fishing boats. We arrived at the same time as one of the fishing boats, so we watched it being winched up the wharf by means of the mechanical chain. I could imagine that boats had been winched up in that way for many, many decades.

Bren then gave us the guided tour of the small fishing hamlet based on the scenes from Poldark. Being an avid fan of the television programme and of Ross Poldark himself, each time she mentioned his name her eyes glistened slightly.

You could see why they had chosen to film there, as everything was pretty much in place already for what they needed but Bren did let us know that the film company had built some new buildings just for the show and that many of these temporary buildings had remained.

We decided it was getting too hot for much more sight-seeing and we wanted to stop for lunch. Originally we were going to stop at Penberth but the heat was creating a bit of a stink from the rotting seaweed. Therefore we decided to head back up the hill and have our lunch up on the headland.

The climb out of the valley was steeper than we had experienced so far and we were all sweating buckets by the top and had to strip off a couple of layers and wrap around our waists and/ or put inside our rucksacks. The sun was shining brightly and the sea looked fabulous from up here. We were able to look out towards Logan Rock, which would be our next destination.

We enjoyed our mixed sandwiches and drank the drinks sparingly, wondering if we had brought enough with us, as we still had more walking to do and a beach to visit. It was actually quite tranquil up here with the lovely view, warm sunshine and birds singing.

The walk to Logan Rock was lovely in the sunshine, it was September after all and now we had climbed up the steep hill the temperature became slightly more temperate.

Logan Rock was quite a dramatic site. The footpath took you through the earthworks created some time ago in the iron age or possibly post-Roman times to create a promontory fort. You could see why they might use this headland jutting into the sea as a location to isolate themselves from attackers but it was probably not that practical as a long-term haven.

The views along each stretch of coast were dazzling. To the West we could see down to the Minack Theatre on the far side of Porthcurno. Suze had tried to get us tickets for the theatre but because of the restrictions there were limited seats available and every night was sold out during our stay, which was a real shame.

We carried on that way back towards Porthcurno but were planning to stop at a beach that Suze had been waxing lyrical about ever since we had started talking about this trip.

Pedn Vounder Beach could not be reached by the road and even reaching it by foot was not that easy. The main pathway was narrow and winding and in some places, quite precipitous. Just like the other paths we have so far walked, we had to keep stopping to let others pass in a socially distanced way. To date, we had experienced no issues with this new etiquette, everyone was polite and patient, much to our pleasure.

The main issue with reaching the beach was the last descent to the beach itself. As we walked towards the path, I could see why Suze was so excited. We were presented with a wide stretch of white sands easing gently into an azure sea. What caused the problem however, was the climb down the rocks to reach those sands.

We had already passed a couple of people, who were not much older than us, who were coming back as they had decided that the access to the beach was too difficult. When we arrived there were a couple of people ahead of us who were climbing down the steep rocks and trying to work out the easiest way down. Bren looked at it with horror, Suze with delight, while myself and Dannii eyed the descent with some trepidation.

“It’s worth it, just look at those sands!” Called Suze with glee. She went first and had soon caught up with the lady ahead, who was being advised on the best way to get down by her partner. Suze joined in, suggesting the lady put her foot in a particular location in the rock face.

I had not tried to do anything like this since I was a child. The descent was actually quite scary for a middle-aged woman like me with a slight fear of heights. Bren however, was really struggling. Surprisingly, it was Dannii who helped her down, taking her hand and guiding her. I would have helped but was too busy concentrating on my own descent. Suze had already reached the beach and was waiting impatiently.

Eventually the four of us got down and then watched with some apprehension as two young men practically shot down the cliff face behind us.

I had concentrated so hard on getting down the cliff face, I hadn't really taken much notice of the people on the beach. Now I did and I was surprised to see that there were naked people everywhere. Not everyone was, but there was certainly a fair number.

Most were lying down minding their own business but others were walking around or playing in the waves, not paying any attention to their own nudity. Suze looked at Bren and I with glee. She obviously knew it was a naturist beach and had decided to keep that information to herself.

We found a suitable spot two thirds of the way along the beach. Suze and Dannii stripped off straight away and lay naked in the sunshine. I started to struggle with my towel and cossie but looking around I realised that half the people were already naked and no one was looking at me. So eventually I just whipped off my clothes and put on my cossie. I had decided not to go naked, as there were so many people around and it didn't feel right. Bren carried on struggling with her towel and costume until she had changed. I tried to stifle a laugh as I watched her struggle.

I took a surreptitious look around me and was able to see a real mixture of people following the naturist way on the beach. Some older people with suntanned and wrinkled skin, making it look like they had been here on the beach for decades. Others were young and pale, obviously making sure they were safe from the sun's rays even though they were lying naked.

I thought how odd it was that these people would happily lie, walk, and swim naked here on this beach, but if you placed them in an urban situation they would be horrified at the idea of being naked in front of people they knew. But in front of strangers down in Cornwall, it was fine.

Suze and Dannii decided to swim, and Bren and I joined them. They seemed to be enjoying the situation and even more when two young naked men started chatting to them in the shallows of the water.

I feel like I have a lot of life experience, but I still found it difficult to chat with two naked men, especially two younger men like these. Bren ignored them completely and just carried on walking into the sea. The water was lovely and the way the shallow beach allowed you to wade made it even more amenable. I could see why Suze had wanted to come here.

We had a swim, lounged on the beach, had another swim and then the two young men came and lay next to Suze and Dannii. They were both in their twenties and seemed quite enamoured with our friends.

Next time they all took to the water, Bren and I were surplus to requirements. The two girls asked the boys whether they were coming in with them and then played with them in the shallows, never letting them get too close.

It was a very relaxing beach and I soon became inured to the sight of naked people walking past me. As we started to get ready to head back to Porthcurno Suze made deliberate care of winking to the two young men and said “see you boys, it was fun!”

The two young men were practically drooling as we headed back along the beach, while Suze and Dannii laughed to each other.

Dannii grinned at Suze, chuckling, “still got it girl!”

CHAPTER EIGHTEEN

That evening we had another shared meal, but when Bren went to help herself Dannii said “No, wait Bren, we will go first, we don't want some extra sea water with our food!”

She winked at Bren and did a little finger snort, which made us all burst out laughing. Bren went a bit red but she did join in with the laughter eventually.

The next day we walked in the other direction along the coast from Porthcurno. Once more we decided to do a circular walk, so we actually headed inland and started in the direction of St Levan church, which was a lovely little stone church in an old village.

From there we went wrong and headed down to the coast path earlier than planned, but we ended up in the lovely village of Porthgwarra. A bit like Penberth, there was an old fishing wharf which led to the sea but here there was also a charming little tunnel as well, which we just had to walk through to the beach.

Again it was a lovely sunny day and there were a couple of people dipping in the sea but we had decided to swim at another beach at Porthchapel on the way back later. We didn't stay too long in Porthgwarra for now and carried on along the coast.

Once more we had to play the Covid ‘social distancing dance’ along the footpath as people walked towards us along the narrow pathway. But soon we were up on the wide open headland, where people could pass each other with ease.

This area was totally different to everywhere else we had passed. It felt wilder and more open, and there were strange conical outcrops which either looked like nuclear silos or as if a gigantic garden gnome had been buried up to his hat rim. There was also the Coastguard station up on the top of the hill but we didn't stay too long as the wind was blowing strongly.

We carried on to another headland called Carn Barra, with dramatic cliff faces heading down to the azure sea. A couple of climbers were braver than us, clinging to the rocks. The sun was warm but the wind did make it a bit more challenging for them.

We stopped to have our packed lunches on the headland and had to put up with Suze and Bren bickering about the choice of sandwiches. We also spotted the choughs which were a famous inhabitant of this coastline. They are an endangered species of bird but doing fairly well here in Cornwall.

I was beginning to feel quite at home down here. The rugged coastline, azure seas and easy pace were very much to my liking, it reminded me quite a bit of the remote South Hams beaches we had found. However I was not stupid enough to forget that it would be very different in inclement weather, with the Atlantic storms battering the coastline, plus places always do feel different and more exciting when you're on holiday.

The walk back was just as lovely but slightly harder as we found the wind was in our faces this time. We stopped for a cream tea at Porthgwarra. This was our first experience of buying anything on holiday and it was all done very systematically. We went to one window to order and pay, all with masks on of course. Then we went around to another window to wait for our orders to be placed there. We then collected our cream teas and went off to our socially distanced picnic table, keeping over 2 metres away from everyone else.

While the tea wasn't the best, the cream and scones were very nice. Three of us made a point of doing the cream the Devon way around, only Bren reneged as she was a 'blow-in' to Devon and therefore wasn't indoctrinated in this inter-county debate like the rest of us had been.

If you had looked on from afar, it would almost seem like a normal warm, late summer day with everyone on picnic tables enjoying themselves. However there was no interaction between the tables and everyone waited for everyone else when disposing of their plates and rubbish. It was a hint of normality though, something that we all craved.

Feeling very refreshed, we headed off back towards Porthcurno once more along the South West Coastal Path, playing socially distanced hopscotch on the way. Three steps forward, no, there's someone coming, head back to a passing place, let them go by and try again, bugger there's another couple, let them pass..."come on, walk faster!"

This last bit Suze said under her breath as we waited for an elderly couple to pass us but even though the rest of us didn't say it, we were all thinking the same thing.

Eventually we got to a wider and less busy stretch and were able to walk uninterrupted for some time. We managed to reach Porthchapel which was to be our afternoon swim location. It was another beautiful beach, much smaller than Porthcurno or Pedn Vounder but being quite remote, it was also quite quiet despite the lovely day. We realised that another reason why it was less busy was that it was also another one with slightly difficult access. Although much easier to reach than Pedn Vounder, it was still a steep path and a bit of clambering over rocks to get onto the beach itself.

Once more the sands were golden and the sea a bright blue but the waves were quite big. As we were all hot and sweaty from the walk, we decided to get changed immediately and go in. I could tell that Suze was itching to strip off completely but there were a couple of families on the beach ("Why weren't their kids in school?" I thought) so it wouldn't have been right.

As we were feeling quite warm from the walk, the water felt cold getting in but it quickly warmed up. The main problem though was the big waves coming in. The waves were pounding on the beach and then the rip tide dragged your feet back outwards.

Suze showed us how to get in by waiting for one wave and then diving directly into the next one to prevent being buffeted by it. It worked, but soon there was another wave, so I had to pause and repeat. Amazingly, thirty or forty yards out from the beach, there was barely any swell or waves and you could swim with ease.

I had got further out than anyone else, but Dannii soon caught up with me, followed by a slightly bedraggled looking Bren and Suze. Bren didn't often get her head under water so she wasn't used to this diving into waves. Soon she calmed down though and we had a lovely swim, enjoying the clear water and warm sunshine.

Dannii was first to start heading back in, but for some reason she didn't get straight out and kept bobbing about in the waves. The three of us looked at each other and decided to head back in just as Dannii finally went through the crashing waves and got to the beach before being knocked over by an incoming swell.

I soon realised what the problem was as I couldn't get into shore either. Each time I swam forward with one wave, it would crash on the beach and then drag me back again. I could see the same happening to Bren, but Suze just ducked her head under and swam strongly to the beach and got out, albeit a bit unsteadily.

I tried to copy her but found it really hard work and soon took in a mouthful of water as the wave crashed around me. Suze and Dannii watched from the beach as Bren and I struggled in the waves. Soon I was beginning to get tired. I looked over and could see that Bren was struggling even more than I was, her head was barely above the water now.

Suze was shouting something from the beach but there was no chance of hearing her. I decided to make one last effort to try and get in and went full pelt with the wave and started doing a rare bit of front crawl. I reached the beach but once more got dragged back and under the waves this time. I took in another mouthful of sea water in my mouth and had no control over my body.

This time however, I didn't get dragged back quite as far and when the water receded I was left on the sand but almost immediately I was hit by another wave from behind and thrown under, once more taking in another mouthful of water. Once again the water receded and I was left on the sand and further in this time. I felt two arms under my shoulders and I was dragged up the beach just as another wave pounded in. The person saving me was knocked over but only temporarily as the wave receded again.

I could barely move but tried as hard as I could to stand up as the arms got under my shoulders once more. Finally, I staggered up the beach, with the support of someone else and collapsed at the feet of Dannii who had been my saviour.

I rolled over in exhaustion. I had never experienced anything like that on a beach. My head was spinning and I started coughing and spitting sea water until I threw up. I could hear Dannii say “Better out than in.” but then she was gone.

I flipped over on to my back, still coughing and panting, to look down the beach and could see that Suze had dived in to help Bren. Bren's head was down in the water as Suze swam alongside her and dragged her sideways rather than towards the shore. Even being encumbered with Bren, Suze was a more powerful swimmer than the rest of us. Dannii followed the progress of Suze and Bren swimming parallel with the sea shore. Suze obviously had a good reason for swimming sideways.

I watched as she waited for the right time and then swam powerfully forward with her legs kicking and one arm dragging her and Bren forward.

Even with that strength she couldn't get all the way in and waited for the next wave before repeating the exercise. This time they reached the beach and Dannii dashed forward and grabbed Bren, hauling her up the beach as Suze got dragged back into the water again. I tried to get up to help but felt dizzy and fell over again in a fit of coughing.

Looking up once more I could see that Suze had made it to shore and was panting heavily but still helping Dannii drag Bren up the beach and back towards where I lay. I looked at Bren with some worry and could see that she was not breathing and had turned ashen white. “Oh shit!” I thought “Don't let Brenda be dead,” but even as I thought this, she suddenly coughed, threw up and started breathing heavily. Suze put her into the recovery position and Bren threw up once more. The clotted cream tea was not staying down too long for either of us.

Suze collapsed onto the beach herself while Dannii kept an eye on Bren. Finally after about a minute someone else from the beach came over to see how we all were. Not really the best advert for community spirit.

Suze said, “oh, we’re all fine and dandy, thank you.” The chap nodded and walked away back to his partner.

“Actually how is everyone?” Asked Suze.

“Fine and dandy,” said Dannii with a tired smile.

“I'm probably just fine, not very dandy at the moment.” I said, trying to laugh but only setting myself off coughing again.

Bren said nothing but did give a thumbs up. I wondered if she couldn't talk or was wary of joining me in a coughing fit. The colour had returned to her cheeks but she didn't look like she was ready to get up or move too far yet.

For the next five minutes or so, we all just lay on the beach breathing heavily. Dannii then wandered back to our bags and brought our drinks over. We all sipped carefully. Dannii and Suze had now recovered completely as they hadn't had the trauma that we did. I was feeling a bit heady but could now start to contemplate standing up.

Dannii walked over to Bren and asked if she was ready to stand, which she did with a little bit of help. So we returned to our bags and towels and stayed there for another hour as we all recovered. Fortunately the sun was so warm on our bodies that we weren't feeling cold, so there wasn't any immediate need to get changed out of our cossies.

I kept my eye on Bren but she seemed to have recovered too. She was drinking her water and looking around the beach with interest once more. I had been really concerned about her immediately after she was pulled to the beach but it does show how resilient the human body can be.

I asked Suze why she had swum sideways. "When there is a riptide, the best way to get out of it is to swim sideways to escape the rip. I thought it was just big waves, like we had at Porthcurno when we got in but this was a proper ripper. Sorry ladies, I would have told you what to try and do."

We all looked at her with a mixture of tiredness and gratitude for what she had already done for us.

Eventually we all got changed once more and apart from the climb from the beach back up to the footpath, the journey wasn't too harsh and we weren't too far away from getting back to the apartment. We were all keeping an eye on Bren, so much so that she eventually shouted out "look, I'm fine, stop worrying!"

We all walked on in silence and then she said again, more quietly this time, "I'm sorry everyone, thank you for saving me back there. I wouldn't have gotten out without you."

We all just shrugged. I hadn't actually done anything as I was too busy saving myself.

Finally we got back to the apartment and all slumped onto the sofas in the living room. Suze then insisted on phoning 111 and putting Bren on the line. She talked through everything that had happened and was told a doctor would call back. Within a few minutes the phone went and Bren answered, going through everything once more. The doctor seemed to be happy with her responses and she suggested that Bren just keep an eye on things and call back immediately if anything got any worse.

Suze blamed herself for letting us all go in in those conditions. But we replied that we were all consenting adults and without Suze being there on the beach Bren probably wouldn't be here now.

Suze kept saying, "if I hadn't been there, you probably wouldn't have gone in though."

To which Bren replied, "yes I bloody well would have. I was hot and sweaty and dying to go in. So just take the thanks, because without you and Dannii I never would have got out".

"I've learned a lesson here today." She said finally.

To be honest I think we all had. The sea can be lovely to look at and swim in but it can also be very dangerous and its power is not to be underestimated.

The meal that evening was more sombre than the previous nights, though Suze tried to lighten the mood by deliberately dripping sea water from her nose. Everyone smiled and we all went to one of the showers, bent over and let the sea water drip from all of our noses. Not one of those things you could explain to a non-swimmer or surfer but it did entertain us all for a minute or two. Bren must have taken in a lot of water as she was there the longest.

We decided to watch one of the DVDs which had been left by the apartment owners for our entertainment. Watching Julia Roberts and Richard Gere in *Pretty Woman* did lighten our hearts a bit and we all got a tear in our eyes when she went back into the snobby shop and showed them the expensive clothes she had bought elsewhere. Just the tonic we needed.

Despite the lift we all got from the film the previous night, none of us felt like swimming the next day, which was to be our last in Cornwall. We all went for a walk on the beach after breakfast and paddled but nothing more.

We had to be out of the apartment by 11am, so we had decided to head back early and stop at the Eden Project on the way back. We checked online, which was fortunate, as you had to book in advance and we were able to book a slot at 1pm.

We arrived at 12:30 and everything was carefully coordinated to take us through the attraction in a safe and secure way. It was a long walk from the car park to the site and some people were complaining about it but for the four of us, it was nothing and it was a nice day, so we enjoyed it as part of the day out. There was quite a wait to get in and once in, we did have to go at the speed of everyone else which was not perfect.

We all wore masks and used the antibacterial hand-wash before entering and then were led through, almost as if on a conveyor belt. In spite of the restrictions, it was still an amazing trip. John had never been interested in visiting, so it was my first trip and I was not disappointed.

We entered through a side door and followed the one way system through the first biome, before being led outside to follow the path to the second biome. Some people were voicing their disappointment at the attraction, the cost and the long queues but we all found it very interesting.

The Rainforest Biome was definitely the highlight but all the way around were amazing plants, artwork and lots of really useful information. I know it wasn't cheap but I think lots of the people were expecting to be transported into a tropical jungle, with lions and tigers and bears ...oh my!

It was quite tiring, so we did enjoy an overpriced coffee and cake for a late lunch before making the trek back up the hill to the car park.

We were all back home by 6pm, after having a lovely, if sometimes challenging weekend. I was really on a high. My friends were so lovely and we had been very lucky with the weather, which enabled us to swim more than we had expected.

However, as I started to unpack, the loneliness of my solitary living conditions hit me even harder after the high of the long weekend. There was no-one here to greet me. I didn't have much food in the house, so I had to drag a frozen pizza out for tea and eat it on my own in front of the telly.

Once more I resorted to a film and this time I put on *Kind Hearts and Coronets*. A bit of killing of one's family seemed in order. The deadpan delivery of Dennis Price was always exquisite, as was Joan Greenwood's innate coolness but of course Alec Guinness stole the show.

I started to feel better after the film but then when I went to bed on my own once more, I bemoaned my current lonely existence.

CHAPTER NINETEEN

26th May 1921 - Lemoncombe Beach, South Devon

Bert was later getting to the beach today. As organised on the previous day, he had arranged to go and visit Mrs Sandford and some other tenants.

First he met with two of his tenant farmers on the edge of Dartmoor to discuss plans for changes to the properties in which they lived, however he was not up to speed wurg sine if the things they asked for and therefore not able to give them the time and reassurances they so desperately needed. Perhaps Tuck was right, he did need an Estate Manager.

Next he went to see Mrs Sandford in a little village called Highweek. She was a strong looking woman but short. She barely came up to Bert's shoulder and her stooped posture made her appear even smaller.

She nodded at Bert as he entered her house and he could see that it was well maintained and spotless. He wished that some of his other tenants were as scrupulous with their cleanliness.

"Oh Mr Windyett, I am so sorry. I have really been struggling to make ends meet since my Edward was killed but now that i have this extra work I am able to start repaying you, though it might be a little bit of time before I am able to catch up."

Bert could see that she was trying her best and he had heard about many people in the same position who did everything they could to stop them being forced to enter the Workhouse.

"I've been to see Mr Tucker" said Bert. Mr Tucker owned the timber yard in which Edward Sandford had been killed by some falling wood last year. "He acknowledges that he should have supported you more after your husband died and he has agreed to pay your rent for the last year. With that in mind, you are now six months ahead of your rental payments, so you can save the money you have and put it towards other things you need. Hopefully this will enable you to keep on top of your payments, maybe give up one of the jobs and make sure your children are still well provided for. If you ever have any more issues with repayments, just get in touch with me and we will discuss it again."

Mrs Sandford was a strong, stoical woman but she almost broke down in tears before Bert. Almost, but not quite, her Victorian upbringing made her keep her emotions in check, though she did say to Bert with a slight tremble in her voice.
"Oh Mr Windyett, thank you. I am not sure how we would have coped otherwise. You are a saint."

Bert thanked her and quickly left, he enjoyed her company but was not one for receiving too much enthusiastic praise. He also felt a strong desire to head home and go down to the beach.

By the time he had got back home and changed his clothes accordingly, it was nearly 5pm when he headed down to the beach. It hardly seemed worth it but something told him it was necessary and whatever it was he was waiting for was imminent.

As he always did when he came down, he scanned the beach first and saw no one. Then he scanned the water, why he was not sure, it was very rare that people swam here apart from the weekends in the summer. There were also no fishing boats any more at Lemoncombe, it was not a natural spot for bringing your boat in, though some fisherman did cast lines from the rocks. Not today though, the whole beach and water was empty.

Bert felt disappointed, he had seemed to think that today was the day. Whatever that meant.

After two hours of waiting to see if things changed, he headed back up the steps to his home. Once more to spend an evening on his own, missing his dead wife and having no company to share his thoughts and deeds with.

CHAPTER TWENTY

October 2020 - Teignmouth

Over the next few weeks we continued to swim but less regularly. I wasn't sure how long I would keep going during the winter months but Dannii and Suze were trying to get me to continue all the way through. Surprisingly for me, the water in October wasn't that cold and it often felt warmer in the water than out, though we did take a trip to Sharrah Pool up on the River Dart and it felt much, much colder. Though that might have been down to the grey skies when we got out.

Bren wasn't coming swimming with us now. She had been knocked by the troubles in Cornwall and hadn't built up the courage to come back in yet. It was a shame as we had got used to the four of us swimming together. The weather started to get worse too, so that might have dissuaded her from returning as well.

It was now over six months since the first lockdown had started and suddenly we looked like we were going the same way again. Everyone was blaming the universities and the students. To be honest it was a bit of a no-brainer, taking people from all over the country (and sometimes the world) and throwing them all together in close confinement. It was pretty much a perfect breeding ground for viruses.

Some local lockdowns were also introduced, in some cities and areas where the rates had risen, many which had nothing to do with students or universities. Once more we became aware of the 'R' rates and everyone became worried as it started to rise above '1' once more. The Labour Party and SAGE called for a two week 'circuit breaker' but the Government decided against it. Instead they brought in different tiers of restrictions and unsurprisingly Devon (and most of England) was in Tier 1. Tier 1 was classed as "medium" but also, somewhat confusingly, the lowest level of restrictions.

However, despite these actions taken, infection rates continued to rise and rise and the death rates followed, so much so that at the end of October Boris announced another national lockdown to start on Bonfire Night.

The new lockdown was very different from the first. Of course, people were still socially distancing and there were definitely more masks around than the first lockdown but otherwise people seemed to be carrying on like they had done for the last few months. I reverted to my one walk and/or swim a day but whereas in the first lock down I wouldn't see many cars or people, now they seemed to be everywhere. Where was everyone going and what were they doing?

Once more I had to stop working. This time it hit me harder than ever. At least in the first lockdown I had the financial support, if not the emotional support, from John. Now I was alone, both financially and emotionally. If it wasn't for my swimming, I think I might have lost the will to live.

I now swam in the sea in November for the first time ever and it was lovely. The buzz I got afterwards was just what people said it would be. A totally different experience and feeling to swimming in the summer. It was all about that first bite of cooler water when you swam and then the blood rush you get afterwards. The only faff was getting changed in the cooler air after the swim. I was following Suze and Dannii's lead and not wearing a wetsuit. My neoprene hat and gloves were fantastic but otherwise I was just wearing my cossie.

Both Suze and Dannii were sporting new drying robes for the post swim. They had both gone for the camouflage pattern robes with the pink lining, so they looked like a very odd pair of twins. One tall, sleek and dark skinned and the other voluptuous and pale skinned. I envied them, as the robes were far out of my price range at the time. I had adapted an old dressing gown and was using that instead. No-one seemed to care or comment on it but I was very self-conscious about it.

Away from the swimming, all people seemed to be talking about was whether we would be able to meet up with friends and families for Christmas. Of course this didn't matter to me at all, and the amount of talking about it seemed totally over the top. Because I had never had a large family, Christmas was not as big a deal as it was for others, so this hysteria about whether you might not be able to see family members on one specific day seemed slightly OTT.

Plans were being made to lift the lockdown on the 2nd December but to bring back the tier system. Devon was placed in Tier 2 along with most of England (to complicate things Wales, Scotland and Northern Ireland had their own systems), many regions up in the North of England were in Tier 3 and only Cornwall and the Isle of Wight were in Tier 1.

Lockdown ended and I was able to start working again. With the run up to Christmas, plus the worries about close contact, I found that I had some regular clients who had been waiting to see me but no new ones were coming in. This meant that I had less money coming in than I had anticipated which hit my chances of bouncing back after lockdown.

One thing that did bounce back after the ending of lockdown was the 'R' rate. During lockdown, rates had been falling across most of the country but almost as soon as lockdown ended, they were rising again.

I continued to swim and the water got colder, Slowly I started wearing boots too and to wear thicker clothing after swimming. I even started taking a washing up bowl with me to the beach.

Now bear with me, I wasn't going mad, there was a good reason. This had been suggested to me by one of the other ladies we sometimes saw at the beach. After swimming, I would put some cold water from the sea into the washing up bowl and then add some boiling water from the flask that I had brought with me. I would then take off the boots and stand in the tepid water while getting changed, slowly adding more boiling water from time to time. This kept my core warm and stopped me getting such a chill. It might look a bit mad but it definitely worked.

However the only drawback was that it added to the amount of stuff we had to take with us when heading for an ever shorter swim. Soon we were spending more time getting changed than swimming and it wasn't so easy to sit on the beach and chat, especially on days with a cold wind. In fact, the cold wind days were the worst and sometimes left me chilled to the bone.

But what a buzz!

The effects of the cold water and the after-swim glow which came when you put on warm clothing and had a hot drink was what made it all worthwhile. I had found that my lined boots and mittens made a massive difference to my feet and hands, plus I had found a Lapland style hat with ear flaps which also helped get me warm post-swim.

A year earlier I couldn't have imagined swimming in the sea in November and December but now it was a regular thing. I had even started swimming with a few different people. It first happened when Suze was busy with work and Dannii had caught Covid. I was at a loss and wasn't sure whether I should swim alone, especially in the winter.

Then I saw a lady posting on the Devon Wild Swimming

Facebook group that she was swimming at Dawlish Warren the next day and would anyone like to come along. I replied and then I joined her and three other ladies for a swim. It was great to do something different. Different routines and company were quite refreshing. Plus I don't think I had actually swam at Dawlish Warren since I was a little girl as it was not a beach favoured by Suze and Dannii and therefore had not been on my radar.

Soon I was following other invitations on Facebook and found some other beaches that I hadn't swam from before or for many years. Sometimes Suze and Dannii would join too but Bren had still not rejoined us and probably wouldn't be now that the temperatures had dropped. We made new friends and many of them would start to message me directly via WhatsApp, making swims possible.

I soon found I was swimming three or four times a week which, apart from our Cornish holiday, was more than I had been doing than any time, even more than in some parts of the summer holidays. I was able to do this by seeing clients in the evening and swimming during the day. For the first time I was affected by the nights drawing in and the fact that we couldn't swim in the evening, therefore the daytime swims were a godsend.

Another bright spot in December was the first Covid Vaccination in the UK. A 90 year old lady was given the jab and soon the most at risk people were being called in to have their first vaccination. Perhaps the end to the bloody pandemic would not be far away.

CHAPTER TWENTY ONE

The Government decided to create a Covid amnesty for Christmas Day, allowing people to travel and mix in bigger groups than normal. This seemed to assuage some of the hysteria but some people suggested it should be for the whole Christmas and New Year period but Boris would not commit one way or another on that.

Normally in mid-to-late December there would be lots of Christmas parties and gatherings but this year that didn't happen. Therefore I was almost surprised when Christmas Day arrived. In fact, it caught me completely off guard. I was alone, no family, no partner and no friends. Suze went visiting her sister for the day and Dannii was with her parents and the rest of her family. It was probably the most depressing Christmas Day I could remember.

It was my first Christmas morning alone and the main thing was the lack of one person to concentrate on. John and I would buy lots of little presents for each other and do stockings, though it was normally me who arranged most of it. This year I had no one like that to buy for and even though I had some friends who gave me gifts, it wasn't quite the same and the only family I had left were quite distantly related and we didn't keep in touch.

On Christmas Day itself, I didn't bother getting dressed and stayed in my PJs all day. I ended up going to bed at about 8pm and watching crappy telly alone for the rest of the evening before finally calling it a day at 10:15pm.

I tried to work out where it had all gone wrong and whether there was any prospect of a better year ahead but there didn't seem to be. My life was in a rut, I had no money, no house and no special someone.

The wider news got worse as lots of the country returned, after the Christmas Day amnesty, to tighter restrictions and the Covid rates soared once more. On the 30th December even Devon joined in with the second highest level of restrictions as it joined Tier 3. Following on from the high of the Christmas celebrations, the damp squib that was the New Year's Eve seeing in of 2021 was probably even more depressing.

For much of 2020 we had looked at 2021 as the year when everything would "get back to normal" - whatever that was to be. However as we marched into 2021, it seemed that we were practically back to square one once more. On the 4th January, Lockdown 3 was announced with rules similar to those of March 2020. Were we ever going to be free of this virus, which seemed to keep bouncing back and biting us in the bum?

The one bright light in the darkness was the vaccination program which continued apace but I found out I wouldn't be getting my first jab until the summer, unless things changed drastically. Perhaps things weren't going to get better as quickly as we all felt a month ago.

January turned out to be a colder month than any of us expected, making swimming much harder than it had been in December. I continued to use warm hats, gloves and now also had a second hand dry robe. Another lady on the Facebook group had got a new one for Xmas and was offering her barely used one for sale. I couldn't really afford it but it turned out to be one of my best investments, as I used it much more than any other item of clothing, since I tended to wear it from the car to the beach and all the way home too!

I continued to swim with different people from the Facebook groups, mainly at Teignmouth but also at Holcombe, Dawlish and other local beaches. However with Holcombe and some other beaches I soon learned to check the Surfers Against Sewage app because there seemed to be way too many sewage discharges into the sea at some of my favourite beaches. How disgusting was that in the 21st Century?

One of the nicest things about swimming with different people was how lovely they all were but also their different journeys to wild swimming. Some, like me, took it up during the first lockdown, others more recently as word started to spread. But some people have been wild swimming for years.

These people became our gurus, they knew what it is like to swim all year around. They also seemed to know more about the sea conditions, tides, sewage, etc, etc. So we would constantly ply them with questions, which they seemed to take with much equanimity.

One lady called Jo, in her early sixties, had had a double mastectomy a few years previously and seemed to be impervious to pain, which she illustrated by swimming in just a swimsuit even in January. I felt like I was pressing her sometimes with questions but she seemed not to mind and was happy to share her love with others. Her own husband would not think of swimming in the sea in the UK in the middle of the summer holidays, let alone January, so she had been swimming alone for years but had found the new uptake in swimming to be fantastic.

Jo took us for a swim at Ness Beach, Shaldon. It was always a bit of a magical mystery tour walking through the dank tunnel and then emerging into the daylight at the other end, even on the cold and cloudy January day we decided to swim there.

There were six of us swimming there together on that occasion. None of us knew each other a few months ago and only Covid and swimming has brought us together. For me this was one bright spark in my otherwise depressing life.

As well as myself and Jo, there was Caley, a twenty year old student, two sisters Jean and Sian, and a totally mad (but fun) lady called Katee. There was already a robust-looking lady on the beach who had just been swimming but when Jo said “Hi Truly,” she was totally ignored.

Jo explained that this lady hated the fact that more people were taking up sea swimming and she felt that beaches like Ness were practically her own private domain because she had been swimming there for the past few years.

“The irony is,” continued Jo, “that she only moved to Devon a few years ago and now she is telling locals and newbies alike that she has more of a right to this beach than they do.”

Jean said, “how rude, I just don't get people like that. Most of the people you meet swimming are so friendly and welcoming.”

Caley nodded. “I’ve been welcomed by so many people since I started. Which is great because none of my friends have shown any interest in joining me. In fact they all think I am absolutely crazy!”

We all laughed.

The friends I was making swimming were papering over the cracks in my life. I loved the camaraderie and friendship but my life seemed to have gone off the rails and it was soon to get worse.

CHAPTER TWENTY TWO

I know the day that the first snow of the winter fell because that was the day that I was given one month's notice on my flat. My landlord had been told by all his friends that if he let out the flat as a holiday let, he would make a lot more money. I was therefore surplus to requirements.

The reason for this was the growth in "staycations". Unable to safely travel abroad, Britons decided to holiday in the UK, and where better than the Devon coastline?

Landlords and property owners all over Devon were starting to let their properties or rooms for the first time and making a killing. It wasn't just the summer holidays either, the season seemed to have extended as people wanted to grab the opportunities of holidays when they were able to. No-one was sure when the next lockdown might appear, so it was best to go away and enjoy their holidays as soon as they could. The demand for holiday properties made my landlord realise that I was better out than in.

This gave me one month to find a new flat, which normally would not be too much of an issue but this year, everyone seemed to have the same idea as my landlord. Every spare room and apartment was being let out on *AirBnB* or other holiday sites. I got all excited when a suitable apartment in Teignmouth became available but when I called the letting agent they told me there were another twenty enquiries already. Suffice to say, I was unsuccessful with my application for that property and for others.

February turned out to be a really negative month. The weather was poor, so we didn't do much swimming. I cut my hand, which meant that I had to cancel some treatments and of course, I failed to find somewhere new to move into.

What was I going to do?

If I couldn't find a new flat, where would I live?

Visions of homelessness and living on the street invaded my thoughts at night. I don't think I had ever felt so low as I did then. There seemed to be no light at the end of the tunnel. I had made six more phone calls in the previous week to try and find a new tenancy but with no success.

Out of the blue, Suze gave me a call and said that I could use her spare room. It was not an ideal scenario for either of us but right now it felt like a lifeline to me and I was really grateful.

I moved out of my flat and into Suze's house on the 14th March. Suze made a joke or two about getting me into her house a month after Valentine's Day which did lighten the situation somewhat.

In fact for the first week or so, it was actually quite pleasant staying with Suze. I quite enjoyed having company again in the evenings, someone to share food with and of course days out walking and swimming.

It might sound a bit like our lives were dominated by walking and swimming and that was partly true but at that point it was much the same for many people in the country. Gyms, spas and swimming pools were open once more but not as busy as they had been pre-Covid, as people still preferred to do their activities and exercise outside where possible.

Wild swimming had probably become the fastest growing pastime in the country. Every week on the Facebook groups we had newbie swimmers asking about going wild swimming for the first time. Plus new groups were popping up all the time too. I started to feel more like a veteran than a newbie and some of the ladies we went swimming with were looking to me for advice and knowledge.

At the end of March there was a warm spell and the numbers on the beaches grew even more. The problem with warm weather in March was that the air temperature might be hot but the sea temperature was at its coldest. So many people got caught out by this as they ran into the sea and felt the freezing cold water. The one positive being the warm air when they got out again. On the warm days, I started to ditch the boots but kept on my gloves and hat. The nicest thing was lying in the sun on the beach after the swim, sometimes it almost felt like summer. This only worked when there was no wind, as soon as the wind picked up, we were reminded that it was March and not July.

Suze showed her experience again and we headed up onto Dartmoor to swim in the more remote lakes and rivers, which sometimes warmed up a bit more quickly than the sea did on warm, sunny days. In one week we went to Foggintor Quarry, Cullever Steps (which was absolutely freezing), Salmon's Leap and Crazywell Pool.

The weather was lovely, the water was getting warmer slowly and it was delightful sitting out on the grass or river banks after the swims, to dry naturally in the sunshine.

During this time we kept to the new friends we had made over the winter and a few newbie extras who were friends of theirs. There were now about a dozen of us who regularly swam together. Normally there were only four or five of us on each swim but when we announced the Crazywell swim one weekend, we had twelve of us meeting in the car park near Whiteworks.

It was a gloriously sunny day and when we reached the pool, we already found half a dozen people there and another group of four people arrived from the direction of Burrator reservoir. It was very different to our previous visit there. It was still a lovely swim but it was too busy for us to enjoy the pool as we would have liked, so we all decided that we would go in smaller groups from now on and probably not to swim at places like this at the weekend.

On the Covid front, the vaccines seemed to be making a difference. Although cases were still high, the number of deaths from Covid were dropping week by week. Talking about vaccinations, I had my own first jab on the 20th March, much earlier than I had expected. Whatever I felt about the large number of mistakes our Government had made during lockdown, the vaccination program seemed to have been a remarkable success.

The jab was quick and efficient and I felt fine afterwards. But that evening I went to bed early feeling tired and the next morning I felt really ill. I was shivering and shaking and I just wanted it to end. Which it actually did later that day. I was so pleased and grateful, thinking if that was the effect of the vaccination, what must the actual virus be like?

CHAPTER TWENTY THREE

March turned into April. Suze was really kind but I could tell she was beginning to weary of having her house invaded by me. Dannii volunteered to put me up for a week, to give Suze a break which was great for Suze and it was nice to spend some time with Dannii in Exeter, but it did feel like I was living out of a suitcase.

Ever since I had lost my flat, even though i had been using my living room, I was wondering how I would be able to manage my clients without a treatment room. I decided I would have to visit my clients armed with my massage bed. For many this made no difference as I had been doing that anyway but this had lost me some clients who either didn't have the space for a treatment or weren't sure about having someone do it at home rather than in a professional treatment room.

On the 12th April, lockdown rules were eased in England (and the other home countries) meaning that non-essential shops could open once more and hairdressers and people like myself could start operating again.

My money was already low and it was probably only thanks to staying with Suze that I was able to survive. I paid her rent but not as much as I would be paying in my own place, plus the shared food and energy costs had been helping a bit too.

Despite this, I was still keen to find my own place but the

number of available properties was getting smaller and smaller. The news was still encouraging people not to holiday abroad this year, so the limited property market in South Devon was being dominated by holiday lets more and more, as people (quite understandably) sought to cash in on the staycation market.

Someone mentioned that they knew of a flat available up towards Taunton but by the time I mulled over the decision of moving so far, it had gone.

On the Covid front, India was seeing a massive increase in the number of cases. The television pictures were very distressing, as masses of people sought help and lines of bodies were burned on mass pyres.

On the 19th April, the Government announced that India would be added to the "red list" on the 23rd April. Unsurprisingly, there was a mass scramble for people to get back from India before the ban was imposed. I felt really sorry for those people who wanted to get home but it seemed crazy to allow such freedom of movement from a Covid hot spot.

Probably even more unsurprisingly, the rates of infection from the "Indian" (later named the "Delta" variant) shot up in areas with large Indian populations in the UK, following this scramble for UK residents to get home. This new variant seemed to be spreading more quickly than the existing "Kent" (or "Alpha") variant.

I found myself going into my shell even more, which was a bit counter intuitive in April and May. Normally spring brought about a fresh start for me, with the longer days, nicer weather and the budding growth of so many plants.

I no longer had a garden to grow plants in, I no longer had a house or even a flat of my own. My work was struggling and the only thing I felt grateful for and that stopped me getting too maudlin, was the fact that I hadn't yet caught Covid and in reality there were a lot of people much worse off than me.

The swims were good fun and with the water and air temperature getting warmer, they were so much more pleasant too. We still got a bit of the cold water buzz from the sea water which was as cold in early May as it was in November but the difference was the air temperature afterwards. It was so much more pleasant to stand around and chat afterwards without having to dash to pull on thick clothing or shivering in the cold wind taking off gloves, hats and boots. I even started wearing my sandals again which was lovely. I kept on taking a hot drink with me and also I kept my dry robe, more for modesty than warmth now.

By the middle of May I was making a concerted effort to find somewhere to live and eventually was able to find a one bedroom apartment in Dawlish but was then told that it had already been let to someone else. My heart was beginning to give up.

Suze and I did manage a long walk on Dartmoor and a swim on a sunny day. She explained that we would be heading towards Red Lake, a remote quarry that had filled with water and created an ideal swimming spot in the middle of Dartmoor. We both took rucksacks, mainly to carry food and drink, as Suze reckoned it was a good 5 miles hike in each direction over some quite rough terrain in places.

We parked up in a popular tourist reservoir car park but while most people were heading up a tarmacked footpath to a popular reservoir, we headed up a steep bank and were almost immediately onto the wild moor and away from the madding crowds.

Our pathway was to follow an old stone tramway which led across the moor. The sun was beating down so we both had thin scarves over our heads and shoulders but these soon got hot and sweaty.

Suze was a lot fitter than I but I was still a good walker and we made good pace. We stopped at a small, old ruined building in the middle of nowhere for lunch. We had both brought sandwiches, which had become a bit squelchy in the warmth of our bags but they were still edible, even if they weren't that robust.

What the building was doing in the middle of nowhere I wasn't quite sure but you could see the site of our destination in the distance and it was marked by a conical hill, which couldn't have been natural. I would later find out that the area was a key kaolin mining area a hundred years earlier and up to 200 men would be working the mine. You wouldn't imagine that when we were there, we could see for miles and there was not a soul in sight, even on a lovely day like that.

We double checked the location of the lake on Suze's OS App on her phone, confirmed it was adjacent to the conical hill (which looked a bit like a volcano) and headed away from the ruined building and towards our destination.

It turned out to be a lot further than it looked and the path did not head directly in that direction after all, but swung around in a slow arc. This new pathway seemed almost like a motorway in comparison with our previous overgrown routes and we found that we had actually joined part of the Two Moors Way.

We got closer and closer to the volcano-like structure and still we couldn't see any lake. All we could see were rocks and tussocks of grass.

“It must be just over there,” said Suze, pointing to the side of the hill. We walked up there and found that the little lake had dried up in the summer heat. Surely that couldn't be it? We both turned around and were presented with a huge pool of water just over a small ridge. We laughed and made our way down.

We weren't wearing much clothing in the heat and within

seconds, Suze had stripped off and started walking towards the lake.

“Aren't you putting on your cossie?”

“Are you kidding, Liv? There isn’t a soul around, it’s warm in the sun and I'm going to enjoy it. Come on, it’s about time you had a proper skinny dip!”

As I have already said, I was no prude but I did think that Suze had an unnatural interest in going skinny dipping. I looked around again and again but of course there was no one there. That didn’t stop me from feeling shy as I left the safety of my clothes pile and started walking towards the lake.

Suze was already into her waist and then dived forward. The way in was quite shallow so it took a little while until my modesty was protected once more but then I was in.

Suze was right, this was a delightful way to swim in a lake like this. The water was quite cold but lovely and the feel of it directly on my skin, together with the warm sun, made me tingle. I wondered why we all thought there was something wrong with skinny dipping, or something to be embarrassed about.

I knew why. I was always swimming with lots of people around and as I wasn't an exhibitionist or a naturist, I would never have felt comfortable or relaxed about going naked, especially if there were men around. But up here with just Suze and I, it felt like the most natural thing in the world.

I lay on my back while my legs and arms gently kept me in place. Some kind of bird of prey hovered near the shore and I watched it, feeling totally at one with nature.

After a while Suze got out and I followed suit but instead of getting dried and dressed, she lay down her thin travel towel and lay down naked in the sunshine.

“Part two.” She declared. “Now you've done the skinny dipping, you've got the lying naked in the sun bit to do."

I looked at her in disbelief, but she continued.

"Feel the sun on your body and soak up the rays. Though you'd better get on some Factor Thirty first!"

Her dark skin meant that she didn't need as much sun tan lotion as the rest of us. I wasn't pale but in this hot sun, I knew better than to let myself fry.

I rubbed the lotion all over myself and then we both lay down on our backs in the sunshine.

I closed my eyes and breathed gently, enjoying the peace and tranquillity. Suze was right, it did add to the experience of being in tune with nature. The idea of lying naked on a packed beach did not appeal to me but this felt lovely.

After a while, lying in the sun out with no wind we had warmed up again. Therefore, we got up and walked back into the waters which felt even better than the first time.

We then swam around, Suze doing her front crawl from one end of the pool to the other, before we started heading back to shore once more. Just before we got to the shallows a couple, probably in their sixties, came over the brow of the hill and started walking towards the lake.

Suze didn't stop, just stood up and walked naked towards the shore. The man didn't look away but watched on, enjoying the view. His wife however gave him quite a look, so finally he turned away and I quickly slipped out and trotted towards the shore and got the towel around me.

Despite our nudity, the couple seemed to be making no plans to head away from our location, in fact they came closer. This made me feel very awkward and so I quickly put on some clothes again and motioned Suze to do the same.

She rolled her eyes, "Bloody old perv, looking at us while his wife was looking the other way. He would have had a heart attack if he had arrived fifteen minutes earlier while we were lying in the sunshine."

We lay back down but our tranquility and repose had been destroyed by the invasion of the aged walkers. It was not a private area but for a while it had been and the intrusion had brought an end to a very enjoyable chapter.

We still had a long walk back to the car and this time, Suze took us a different way following a new path, so that after 5 miles or so we came down a steep gradient towards Avon Dam and eventually joined the masses on the path laid with tarmac which took us back towards Shipley Bridge.

CHAPTER TWENTY FOUR

As my home life was in turmoil, I decided to upset it even more by trying the online dating world again. I was beginning to feel as if I would like a good man in my life.

Once more I had to trawl through various questions about which picture I preferred or "If your date turned up late what would you say?"

Oh for god's sake, forget all this palaver. Just let me chat to some people and I would know whether I would want to go out with them or not. Saying that, my success rate in the past in picking good men wasn't that great...

Finally I managed to get through to look at profiles and had to learn to "swipe left" or "swipe right". Don't ask me which was which, as I managed to forget every time. For some reason it was showing me men in Wales, until I realised that my settings were set to be up to 90 miles away. I reset it to be more local (I could always extend it later) and tweaked a few more settings before trying again.

There were more local men this time but each time I looked there was something which put me off about them. Whether they were a smoker or said their favourite dinner was roast beef (which for me as a vegetarian was a real put off) or they spent their weekends riding motorbikes, there seemed to be something wrong with all of them.

Then I started to get likes from other men, but was quite surprised that they didn't seem to be my kind of age group. The first couple were in their late 50s and I had already decided to set a limit of 50. Then I got likes from men who were in their early thirties. Perhaps they were looking for a 'cougar'. I wasn't exactly sure what a cougar was, but Dannii talked about older women who enjoyed the company of younger men "showing them the ropes".

After a couple of unproductive days, I decided to try another site but found it very similar. Slowly I decided to "like" a few men and respond to some of the men who had liked me but this was where the real trouble started.

The first man I got chatting to didn't want to talk online but wanted me to send photos to him. Each time, he asked for something even more revealing, and he got quite aggressive when I didn't accede to his requests.

Next came the men who only wanted to meet up for a one night stand. Some were even in relationships though they tried to keep this hidden. One chap did try a bit of honesty "My wife and I are not on the same plane so I am looking for someone I can relate to on a physical level". Although his language was flowery, he was basically saying "I'm looking for some good sex outside of my marriage".

Apparently men looking for a bit on the side was quite common and it seemed there were lots of women who were happy to give them what they wanted. I wasn't one of them though.

Of course I could have been tempted to jump into bed with one of these men but that wasn't really me. The Covid thing at least gave me a good excuse for not seeing them. In all, I tried three different sites/apps and got absolutely nowhere. I wasted so much time but seemed to have no success in finding the right man. There must be nice gentlemen out there somewhere but I couldn't find one.

I had a few online chats with some men but they didn't go anywhere. When I mentioned I was vegetarian, they either tried to justify their meat eating or gave up entirely (one man said "Bye then" and ended the call).

Eventually I gave up, it looked like I was going to be a middle-aged spinster. Living alone and spending more lonely nights with a 1980s film, box of chocolates and multiple G&Ts.

CHAPTER TWENTY FIVE

27th May 1921 - Lemoncombe Beach

Bert walked down to the beach once more dressed in his brown flannel suit. He had brought with him a vacuum flask full of tea prepared by Mrs Holmes. This would prevent one of the reasons he would have for having to head back up the steps to his house. Of course the drinking of tea all morning would also necessitate another reason for heading back to the house but he tried not to think about that too much.

Once more, he had no inspiration for the reason for his need to head down and sit on the beach. He had tried to explain it to Mrs Holmes but she just thought he had lost his marbles. Bert sometimes wondered whether this was actually the case after all.

All he knew was that he had a burning drive to go and sit on the beach and stare out to sea, waiting for something to happen. What that thing was, he couldn't tell you but he also knew that he would know what it was when it happened.

The morning was fresh but not too cold as the slight cloud cover prevented a frost and there was no wind. Bert was warm in his flannel suit and even considered taking off his jacket but decided against it in case anyone came and saw him. The tide was particularly low today and Bert decided to take a turn around the beach before returning to his normal spot on the rocks.

Time passed slowly as he watched the cormorants float and dive in the shallow water. The sun tried to poke through the cloud but failed. A pair of seals appeared for a moment but disappeared again.

Bert enjoyed his second cup of tea and decided to use the open air facilities that the beach provided for the result that two cups of tea had caused.

He was just returning to his place on the rocks when something new did happen. He caught a glimpse of something orange in the near distance out in the sea. It was a very bright orange, not something you would see normally, especially out in the sea.

He didn't know why but Bert started to get excited, perhaps this was the thing he had been waiting for all this time...

CHAPTER TWENTY SIX

27th May 2021 – Lemoncombe Beach

I had heard a lot about Lemoncombe beach but hadn't swum there yet. Suze would come here with some of her other swimming friends because, as she says, "there are usually less bloody kids here." It was one of those hidden coves between Teignmouth and Torquay which was accessible by car but there was no real parking available and still a little walk to the beach, so it was popular with walkers and other people who didn't mind a little trek to the beach. There were also the local residents of Lemoncombe who could walk down to the beach.

I was with Suze and three of her friends, slightly squashed in the back of her 4x4 vehicle. We turned off the main road and headed down a steep and winding lane. Despite the time of year, it was quite dark in the lane with the trees overhanging the roadway. On a sharp bend around to the left, Suze swung over to the right hand side of the road and she practically did a u-turn into a driveway on the left hand side. We drove for about 30 yards before Suze stopped the car in front of some wooden gates which looked a little worse for wear. She got out of the car and I expected her to go and open the gates but the others started getting out of the car too. Suze ducked her head back into the car and called to me "C'mon. Get out, this is where we're stopping."

The others had already reclaimed their bags from the boot and Anna passed my bag to me. I was obviously showing some signs of concern or confusion with regards to parking our car in the middle of someone's driveway but Tessa explained, "the house has been empty for decades. Most people don't know about it but a few of us swimmers do and it's a first come, first served basis. If you're lucky enough to get here first, you can park here and walk down to the beach." She shrugged and started off back down the driveway.

It was definitely a lucky place to park as there were only a couple more houses on the lane before we reached a small lay-by where there was one single car parked. Here there were signs and information boards, showing the two different directions of the South West Coastal Path and the steps leading down to Lemoncombe Beach.

We made our way down the steps and headed to the right hand side of the beach which seemed to be getting the morning sun as the cliffs to the East were shading the left hand side. Suze and the others said hello to a few people who were already getting changed after their swim. Many of the regular swimmers headed down early in the summer to beat the larger numbers that would come down later.

As we walked down we could see that it was a really low tide, making the beach much bigger than normal and also meaning that many people in the sea were standing in the shallows. Suze and her gang were planning to swim around to the next cove and back. Although I could just about do that, I would be much slower than them. So I had decided to stay and enjoy my swim in and around the cove itself.

We found a spot by the rocks in the morning sun where we could leave our things and proceeded to get changed. As the water was warming up, I was no longer wearing gloves or boots but I did wear my fluorescent hat and attached my new bright orange tow float to my waist so I could be spotted by other water users.

Most of the swimmers were swimming on the right hand side of the cove so as to enjoy the sunshine and soon Suze and the other three were heading off towards the 5 knot marker buoy. I knew they were then going to head off towards another buoy in the next cove but I didn't plan to swim that far.

As the other side of the cove was empty, I decided to swim that way. At first I waded through the shallow water but eventually decided to dive forward and swim. Although there was no sun, the water was still mild and the cliffs had a lovely red hue to them. A glint of something caught my eye and I headed in that direction. Once again I got a glint of something and a hint of light blue against the red of the rocks and the dark greens of the foliage on the cliffs.

As I approached the end of the promontory I noticed what it was. There was an archway in the rocks that was probably under the water normally but the low tide had uncovered it. There was about three or four feet of space between the water and the roof of the archway and through it you could see the sky and some of the scenery on the other side. It looked very tempting to swim through to the other side.

Normally I would be frightened of doing something like that, especially on my own but something was drawing me forward. It was obviously only something that appeared on a day with a very low tide. The water was very still and this together with the lovely sunny morning, made it feel much more benign than it might be normally. Although the sea conditions were very light, when I got closer to the rocks, there was a little bit of swirling of currents but not enough to put me off.

As I got closer to the archway, the sun streamed through, glaring in my eyes. I could no longer see any detail but I was spurred forward by some crazy desire to get to the other side. So I swam blindly, hoping that the gap was as real as I had originally imagined and there were no hidden rocks.

Fortunately the tide and current were on my side and I went through with some ease and was soon out the other side. I still couldn't see much as the sun was in my eyes but after a few more seconds, I was able to to make out the coastline and see I was actually in a little inlet bordered on the far side by a low outcrop of rock which the sun was streaming over. As I got closer I was able to get out of its glare, and get a good look around. It was all quite magical, a hidden little world of crimson rocks and azure sea, spattered with creamy white flecks of waves.

The inlet wasn't large, I was only about ten metres from the shoreline here but about thirty metres from the exit. The waves were swirling me around a little, so I decided not to stay too long. I knew I could swim the thirty metres to the exit of the inlet with ease, but I didn't know how far it would be to swim around the headland back to the cove, so I decided to swim back the way I came.

I turned back to the rock face through which I had come but was surprised to see not one but two little archways. What was that about? I was sure there had only been one when I had swum from the other side. But of course there couldn't have been. Perhaps one was hidden from the other side. Which one was the one I had swum through? Looking at them both they looked like they were clear ways back to the cove on the other side but the one on the right, which I was much closer to, looked slightly darker than the other. As the current was taking me that way and I was closer, I decided to swim through there.

Within seconds I was through, with only a little resistance from the tide rather than the current. I was quickly through and breathed a little sigh of relief, the unreasonable concern leaving me again. But as I swam back towards the shoreline, I admonished myself for being silly and creating a problem when there wasn't one.

The sun seemed to have ducked in behind some clouds since I had been swimming in the inlet and it looked like a lot of people had left the beach. I used a mixture of breaststroke and front crawl to make my way back to the beach and head back to the rocks on which the five of us had left our bags and change of clothing. Oddly, there only seemed to be one man left on the beach, sat on the rocks in the middle. He seemed quite formally dressed for the beach in a brown flannel suit, but nothing surprised me any more, especially after the events of the previous year or so.

I turned back to locate my bag on the rocks but couldn't see it or the other bags either. I turned around in a state of confusion. I was sure that we had left them there. I walked around the other side of the rocks, just in case I had forgotten and we actually left them on that side but they weren't there either.

I turned back to look at the sea to see if my friends were on their way back but there was no-one in sight. They must still be at the other cove.

I stood in confusion and then decided to use the only option available to me. I walked over to the gentleman who was sat on the rocks. I was suddenly aware that he was sitting there in full suit whereas I was standing in my swimming costume and beginning to get goose pimples, as the sun had definitely withdrawn behind the clouds for the time being.

The man looked at me in a strange way as I walked towards him, but he stood up as I approached and nodded his head gently. I was about to ask him about the clothes and bags but he interrupted me, asking, “have you swum far? Do you not have something to dry with?”

“Yes, I thought I did. We left our clothes and bags on the rocks over there but when I returned they were gone. Did you see anyone else pick them up?”

He shook his head “You are the only person I have seen on the beach this morning and I’ve been sitting here for over an hour.”

“Now don't be daft, myself and my friends only arrived about half an hour ago and there were quite a few people on the beach and up at the cafe..."

I looked up to where I started to point towards the cafe by the steps but there was no cafe there. I started shaking my head in confusion and also gave a little shiver with the cold.

"Would you like a towel, my house is only a few minutes walk away?"

Bewildered, I looked around myself at the beach and out towards the sea. It looked just like the beach I had arrived at before but there were now no other people, the cafe was gone and I could see there were no railings alongside the steps leading down to the beach. I looked out to sea and there was still no sign of my friends. Perhaps I had become disorientated in that little inlet and came out the wrong way and ended up in a completely different cove.

"What is the name of this cove?" I asked the man.

"Lemoncombe Cove." he replied and I shivered once more.

"I don't understand..."

"Here," he took off his suit jacket and draped it around my shoulders. "Let me find you a towel and I can get you a cup of tea. Don't worry, my housekeeper, Mrs Holmes, is in the house so she can be your chaperone and prevent you from being in a strange man's house unattended."

My confusion continued but I allowed myself to be guided up the steps and soon we were back in the little lane, which didn't seem any different from our recent trip down.

The man turned to me. "Apologies, I have not introduced myself. My name is Bertrand Windyett but most people just call me Bert. And you are?"

It took me a moment for my head to clear before replying, "Olivia Wylde."

"A pleasure to meet you Mrs..." he paused and looked at me inquiringly "Wylde"

"No," I replied. "It's Miss Wylde." I was tempted to use the prefix Ms to make a point but decided against it at the last minute.

"My apologies. It is one of the unforeseen travesties of the war that so many women have been left without men to marry."

He turned and continued walking up the lane, leaving me even more confused than before. What war?

Presently, he turned into the very drive where our car was parked and called over his shoulder, "my house is just a short walk now."

"Oh gosh, apologies. When myself and my friends arrived we parked our car in front of your gates."

Once more he turned, but that time is what his turn to look confused. "You arrived in a car?"

"Yes, my friend Suze parked in front of your gates." But as I looked where I was pointing, I could clearly see that there was no vehicle there. Giving me one more curious look, Bert made his way through the partially open wooden gates.

I shook my head once more and followed him. He must have been beginning to think that I was quite mad. In fact, I was actually beginning to wonder if he could be right.

It was not far from the gate to his house and he quickly opened the door and called out to an unseen person within. A woman came to the door and Bert guided me towards her, explaining that I had come from the sea and needed a warming drink, a towel and a change of clothes.

In the hands of the aforementioned Mrs Holmes, I was guided to a side room where I was given a towel, and a change of clothing was laid out in front of me. The knickers and shift were quite old fashioned and made of silk but quite comfortable to wear. The white dress had lacy frills around the neck and cuffs but it was also light and comfortable. Finally, there were some white canvas slippers and I was dressed once more, though still left unaware about what was happening. Mrs Holmes returned to the room once more and enquired about how I was doing and then asked me to follow her into the 'front parlour'.

Bert was seated on a wickerwork chair looking out of the bay window but got up as we entered the room. "Miss Wylde, I am delighted to see that you are much restored." He indicated towards the other wicker chair. "Please join me. Would you like some tea?" And he indicated towards the vintage tea set.

I nodded and he started to pour some tea into the cups. He picked up the milk jug. "Milk?" he enquired.
"Yes, please." I replied and he poured some into the cup. Next his hands moved to the sugar tongs.
"One lump or two?" he asked.
I hesitated slightly before replying "Oh, none thanks." He looked slightly surprised before placing one lump in one of the cups and handing me the other cup. I took it and sipped at the tea.

Mrs Holmes returned to the room and laid out some small plates filled with neatly cut sandwiches, scones, jam and cream.

Bert said, "help yourself to anything you want Miss Wylde, I think you need some good nourishment inside of you."

"Thank you Bert." I replied. Mrs Holmes turned as I said this and gave me a look of disdain.

As she left the room Bert leant over and said, "she does not think it is proper for a lady to refer to a gentleman by his first name. Especially one of such novel acquaintance."

"Is she a bit old fashioned?" I asked.

"That would be an understatement, Miss Wylde. But she has

been very good to me since my wife died two years ago."

"Oh gosh, I'm sorry to hear that Bert." For some reason I continued, "do you mind me asking what happened?"

"She was taken by the Spanish Influenza in the winter of 1919." he replied.

I nodded my head in sympathy before my brain did a reality check. Did he just say 1919?

"Sorry, when?"

"The 3rd February 1919, I remember it like it was yesterday." he looked down sadly.

Part of me wanted to scream, accuse him of making a joke out of such a serious thing, but something stopped me. My mind flicked back to the changes on the beach, the missing car, the abandoned house which was now occupied. The strange dress and mannerisms of my host and his housekeeper.

Had I somehow ended up in 1919. Actually no, he said *two years ago* so it must be 1921. What the hell was going on?

Was I going mad? Was I dreaming? Or was I actually in 1921?

I tried to remember what time travellers did when they travelled back in time, but all I could remember was Marty McFly kissing his mother and playing Johnny B Goode. Oh yes and the flying cars but that was when he went forward in time. None of that was any help for me in my current predicament.

Obviously, none of this was real. To prove it to myself, I took a fork from the table and stabbed my hand with it. The pain that followed was sharp and very real. Well, it didn't seem like I was dreaming and it had made Bert look at me with some bemusement.

"Sorry, my hand slipped." I explained without any real conviction.

"You are an unusual house guest Miss Wylde, if you don't mind me making the observation?"

I laughed. "No, I can quite understand you thinking that Bert. However I am grateful for your kindness, warm clothes and this food."

"How did you come to be on the beach without any clothes or things to dry yourself with?"

I thought quickly for a suitable answer and said, "I went to the beach with some friends. I think they must have forgotten about me and taken my things as well by accident. In fact, I think I should head back, just in case they come looking for me."

I was beginning to worry about my situation and believed that the sooner I could get back to the beach, the sooner I could resolve whatever the hell was happening and either get back to my own time or wake up from this very realistic dream.

I stood up and Bert instinctively stood up too.
"Of course Miss Wylde. would you do me the honour of letting me escort you to the beach?"

"Oh that won't be necessary." I replied,

"I insist. After all, you have only just regained the colour in your cheeks and we would not want you being overcome again."

I hesitated, but decided not to argue with him, instead saying, "thank you, you are very kind."

And with that we both left the parlour.

CHAPTER TWENTY SEVEN

27th May 1921 – Lemoncombe Beach

On the way down to the beach, I was wondering how I would shake him off, as I wanted to get changed back into my swimming costume, hat and tow float, which Mrs Holmes had presented back to me as if they were a nuclear bomb rather than swimming attire. I think she had even managed to iron and starch it in the time we had taken morning tea.

We returned to the steps and my eyes looked out to sea and then my heart sank. Of course it was a few hours later and the tide had now risen, hiding the cave completely. I wouldn't be able to try and return until the tide had fallen once more, which would be in a few more hours.

Even then, who knew whether I could return to 2021. I turned to Bert, slapping my forehead in mock admonition. "Of course, I remember now. The ladies said they would return later today, probably around 7 o'clock, to take me home."

"Of course." said Bert "And what are you going to do in the meantime? I can arrange for a carriage to take you home if you wish. Where is your home?"

"Teignmouth." I replied, the word escaping my mouth before I could stop it. "No, that is very kind Bert, but my friends would be distraught if they missed me and they might wonder what had happened to me. I think I should stick around and come back again later."

"In that case, would you allow me to escort you back to the house and we can take a turn around the garden together?"

Once again, I didn't know how to say no and I realised that part of the reason was that I liked Bert and wanted to spend some more time with him. Soon we were walking around his garden, which was delightful.

"My wife was the gardener, but since she passed away Mr Holmes has managed to maintain it, just as she left it." There was a look of melancholy in his eye but the garden obviously also brought him joy.

We walked around the garden and stopped from time to time to enjoy the views or the smell of some of the flowers. In that time we found out quite a bit about each other. He and his wife were married for twenty years but she had caught German measles early in her pregnancy and had miscarried. After that, she thought she could not have children and was prone to viruses and infections.

"If anyone was to catch Spanish Influenza, it would be my Doris" he said with sorrow.

My own circumstances were more difficult to explain. I wasn't sure whether it was better to say that John and I had been married and now divorced or whether we had never married. Which was worse in these times?

I eventually settled on having a man who I wanted to marry but he was killed during the war and I had not had a relationship since. It was a lie but only a white lie and seemed to explain my unmarried status to him satisfactorily.

What did surprise me was his understanding of what I did for a living. I tried to explain that I did body work to help people to rehabilitate and then he said, “ah, you are a physiotherapist?”

Not knowing how old the term “physiotherapy” was, I was slightly taken aback. Therefore I just nodded dumbly and said “erm, yes.”

Unperturbed he continued, “many of my comrades were aided after the war by physiotherapists, I still see many of them and not all have proper use of all their limbs.”

He then went silent and contemplative for a moment. I understood and did not press him on his memories of those tragic times.

Mrs Holmes kept us fed and watered and we ended up sitting on the verandah enjoying the afternoon sun. I must admit it was one of the most pleasant afternoons I had spent in a long time.

However I was still a fish out of water and I needed to see if I could return to my own time. I took my leave from Bert around 6pm, explaining that my friends would find it very odd for me to be accompanied by a man I barely knew. He agreed that would not be seemly but he took my hand and kissed it gently.

A little shiver went down my spine.

CHAPTER TWENTY EIGHT

I left the house, which I now saw was called Elm House, as if I was walking on air. I quickly berated myself for letting down women in general and acting like a teenager.

My amusement soon turned once more to trepidation as I made my way down the steps to the beach. I began to get concerned once more about whether I could actually return to my own time or whether this was all some crazy dream and I had actually lost my mind altogether.

I could now see the archway had reappeared and there was definitely only one there, not two as I had seen from the other side. The beach and the sea was empty. I made my way behind some of the rocks and changed out of my borrowed clothes once more into my swimming cossie. I looked around for somewhere to stash the 1920s clothes, just in case I could not return to my own time.

There was a perfect little fissure in the rocks which was created by some softer rocks being weathered away. The place was dry and also hidden from sight, in case anyone else came along that way.

I made my way back to the shoreline, looked around me to determine I was still alone and swam straight for the archway. This time, the sun had made its way around the beach and was now behind me and I could see the archway and the view beyond it clearly.

The swim did not take long and I soon reached the archway. I continued on, swimming straight through. Once on the other side I turned around to face the archway once more and could see the low sun streaming through from the way I had come.

I was again presented with two arches rather than one from this side. However, this time I knew which one I had just swam through and therefore I looked towards the left hand archway and wondered whether it would take me back to 2021. There was only one way to find out. I swam through.

Almost immediately, I could tell the difference. The sun was shining on the far side of the cove rather than directed into my eyes. Then there was the sound of other voices. I looked and could see other swimmers, people on paddle boards and people on the beach. I could have cried with relief!

I made my way back to the beach and headed to where we had left our things, not expecting them to be there. My friends wouldn't have waited around all day for me to return and actually, I now realised, they must be really worried about me as I had probably been missing for ten or eleven hours.

Incredibly my bag was there on the rocks and it was next to some other bags. I stood there in bemusement, until I heard a voice call my name.

"Olivia, where did you swim to?"

I turned and there was Suze and the others walking up the beach, looking like they had just got out of the water.

It soon became apparent that I had not been missing all day. Everything that had happened in 1921 had happened in no time at all. Had I really travelled back in time or had I somehow had a very realistic dream?

The memory of Bert and Mrs Holmes was so real, as was the food and drink. I couldn't have dreamed it all, could I?

Then I remembered my hand and the fork. Yes there were marks that the tines had made when I wanted to test if I was awake or not. Either I had very vivid dreams and acted out some of the things that happened or else I had genuinely travelled back to 1921.

After we had got dressed and enjoyed our drinks, we made our way back up to the car. I glanced at the cafe with some small delight and amusement on the way but when we reached the driveway to Elm House, I gave an involuntary shiver.

It was much more overgrown than I had seen it earlier and the gates were in far worse repair. I peered through the gates but the house was just out of sight around the bend. Part of me wanted to climb up and over the gates and find out whether the house was one and the same but my friends were looking at me confusedly.

I decided to leave that for another day.

CHAPTER TWENTY NINE

27th May 2021 – Teignmouth

I tried to work in the afternoon but failed completely. All I could think about was what had happened to me and whether it was all real or not.

Eventually, after hours of pretending to work, I gave up and resolved to return to Lemoncombe the next day. I prepared myself, picking some suitable clothing which would work in Edwardian times or whatever it was the time period was called back then. I found my dry bag float that I planned to take with me and then settled down to do some Internet searching on 1921, the Spanish influenza and whatever else could help me understand things better.

Part of me was worried that I wouldn't be able to get back there and all this effort would be wasted, but the other part of me knew that it was better to have and not need than need and not have.

The next morning I breakfasted early and prepared multiple drinks and snacks for my journey. I wasn't quite sure why.

I drove over to Lemoncombe and made my way into the now familiar drive leading up to Elm House. I decided to get a quick look at the house as it was now. I actually managed to scale and vault the wooden gates more effectively than I expected to but when I had, a cold shiver went down my spine. What would I find around the bend? Another house? 1921? Some people living there? Or even some guard dogs?

None of these appeared as I rounded the bend though, and there in front of me was Elm House, much as I had seen it just one day (or one hundred years) earlier.

It was dark and the windows were boarded up but it was obviously looked after by somebody, as it looked like it had recently been painted. This wasn't the decrepit house that I had imagined from Suze's intimations. But it was clear that even if someone was maintaining the facade and tidying the gardens from time to time, there was no-one living here.

There wasn’t much more I could learn from the house and I was on a fairly tight schedule if I was to catch the low tide again. I was a bit later than the previous morning but there was no sun, so the beach was quieter today.

I got changed and put my things into the dry bag. I checked to see if the dress that I had hidden in the rock fissure was there, but the fissure was empty, the dress had not travelled in time with me.

I made my way into the sea and headed straight for the archway. Once again I seemed alone in this part of the water and I marvelled at the fact that everyone else seemed to be steering clear of the archway. Perhaps I was the only one who could see it, or something was deterring them from getting too close.

Again the way was easy and this time, with the clouds obscuring the sun, I could actually see through the archway to the other side and I swam through gently. Once again I turned around and was confronted with two archways.

I thought for a moment about what I was doing but quickly overcame any qualms and swam through the right hand archway.

Again, I was presented with an empty sea and my more accustomed eyes could tell that I was back in 1921 as there was no cafe or other signs of modernisation on and around the beach. However there was no sign of Bert this time.

Up until this point, all of my energy had been directed towards discovering whether I had actually travelled to 1921 on the previous day and whether I could return once more. Now my brain started to tick with another incentive altogether.

I made my way straight to the beach and unhooked my dry bag. I took out my clothes and towel and placed them on the rocks. Within minutes I was dry, dressed in a summer dress suitable for 1921 and had enjoyed a warming drink. Even more importantly, I had spent some time getting my hair right, applying some subtle make-up and some organic and natural body scent and eau de toilette. I did not like to admit to myself why I was making such an effort.

I made my way to the fissure and was delighted to discover that the dress, underwear and shoes from the previous day were indeed there. I quickly took them and replaced them with the dry bag and other things I had brought with me. The clothes from the previous day would give me a good excuse to return once more to Elm House.

I made my way up the steps, this time passing a couple who were heading down to the beach. I automatically stopped to let them through, as that is what we did back in ‘Covid Britain’ and they thanked me. I realised I was probably just being as polite as other people in this day and age.

Soon I was back at the gates of Elm House and this time I had to open them to get in. Walking up to the door, I wasn't quite sure how I would alert those inside of my presence but then I saw there was an actual bell on the wall that you pulled a little rope from and it chimed accordingly.

Pretty much straight away (was she waiting just inside?), the door was opened by Mrs Holmes. Despite the fact that I had been there the day before, she showed no sign or recognition and just said "Yes?"

I started to worry, perhaps the events of yesterday hadn't happened to them after all. Who knew how time and events followed on in this strange new time travelling world I had entered. What if I had come back on the same day or a different year altogether?

I decided to proffer the clothes and said, "I thought I should return these to you once more."

This time there was a slight glimmer of acknowledgement from her "Ah, yes, thank you." she said as she took the clothes and shoes.

"Is Mr...umm...Windyett at home?" It took me a moment to remember Bert's surname. I had already realised that asking for "Bert" would not do.

"I will see whether the Master is accepting visitors." She beckoned me into the hallway and left me there, so I took the opportunity to inspect the furniture and paintings.

"Miss Wylde!" Bert walked in, smiling profusely. "I didn't count on having the pleasure of seeing you again so quickly. Please have a seat." He beckoned towards the parlour and one of the chairs as he said this.

"I came to return the clothes you so kindly lent to me yesterday. I am afraid I have not had the chance to wash... launder them as yet."

"That is of no consequence. I am just delighted that you have returned and that I am here to greet you. I am shortly heading out for the day and I wonder whether you would care to join me. I am taking a carriage to Torquay Railway Station and then catching a train to Newton Abbot for the day. There is a band playing in the park and I was hoping to have lunch in the town. Would you care to accompany me?"

I was taken aback. Not only would I have the opportunity to check out places like Torquay and Newton Abbot in 1921 but this man wanted to spend more time with me. I was not quite sure which fact delighted me more.

Within minutes we were ready to leave, the carriage had arrived from a local taxi firm. I was delighted to see that it was being pulled by two horses.

Noticing me looking at the horses, Bert smiled almost shyly. "I know it is not the done thing nowadays but I still prefer horse-drawn cabs to automobiles. Mr Green here is one of the few locally who still operates them." Mr Green doffed his cap and opened the door of the carriage, while Bert held out his hand to help me up first.

I broadly hold feminist views but I do like a bit of old-fashioned gentlemanly manners too!

CHAPTER THIRTY ONE

28th May 1921 – Torquay

The journey through Torquay was a delight. I was not 100% sure of my bearings, as so many of the roads had changed but largely it was just much more pleasant - there were more trees, more green spaces and the buildings were delightful.

However at one point we passed some really run down dwellings and people looking very bedraggled and there was obviously severe poverty here too. It was something I would not forget later on.

The final leg of the journey was the most pleasant though. We travelled along Torquay seafront, where lots of people were walking along the promenade and there were no cars in sight. Torquay seafront looked like something out of Mary Poppins and, I laughed to myself at the thought, I had my own Bert to accompany me too! The last part of the journey took us from the Pavilion to the Grand Hotel, both of which looked like they had had a good clean up. In contrast the railway station was very smoky and grimy.

The reason for this soon became apparent after Bert had bought us two tickets, as a steam train arrived and everything was shrouded in the steam and soot that accompanied it.

We got on the train and entered one of the first class compartments which we had to ourselves. It had been many years since I had sat in a train compartment like this. It all felt a bit like Harry Potter.

Bert and I talked but I couldn't help staring out of the window to enjoy the view as we made our way through the South Devon countryside. There did seem to be a lot of greenery but my minimal memory of train journeys did seem to suggest that apart from the towns and the stations, trains did mainly travel through the countryside, especially in Devon!

The journey didn't take long and soon we were arriving in Newton Abbot. Now we saw a different side, the approach to the station was a veritable warren of industrial action. There was smoke, steam and sparks, just like an episode of Peaky Blinders, but it did seem slightly odd on a warm, sunny late spring day.

On arrival in the station, Bert got up, opened the door and exited before turning to help me out once more. I thought to myself, *I could get used to this.*

This time at the station there was a large number of people all heading to the stairs together. My Covid-world brain was not quite ready for the crowds of people all moving together without any social distancing. A phrase that I had not heard of just eighteen months earlier.

Once more, Bert helped by guiding me through the crowds and up the stairs, along the top walkway and back down the far stairs and out through the station.

We emerged once more into the bright sunlight. Bert checked his pocket watch and said "We have a little bit of time before the band is due to start, would you like to take some tea first?"

"That would be lovely," I agreed. I had a momentary panic when I realised that I had nothing which would pass for money in 1921 but then I realised that Bert was the kind of man who would never expect a woman to pay her way.

We crossed the road to the Queen's Hotel. Now I actually got to see some old fashioned cars as there were a couple parked up and we passed a few travelling along the road too. The noise was awful and the smell of petrol was just as bad. There were also a few horse-drawn vehicles and even one man pulling a cart full of bricks by hand. I couldn't help thinking about the cultural references that I had seen on television or in films and this was just like a scene from a period film.

As soon as we entered the Hotel, I was presented with another film set. The waitresses were dressed in black and lace. The male customers all wore suits and the ladies, elegant dresses. I actually felt a little under-dressed but when we were guided to our table, I relaxed once more.

We spent a lovely half hour chatting and drinking tea from china cups. Bert had remembered my lack of sugar in my tea, which I appreciated. Some men in my life could not remember simple details like that after living together for months.

We got to know each other more. I found out more about Bert's property business which he had inherited from his father, but had grown it to twice the size it was when he received it. I created my own new backstory that I had been orphaned and had no direct family, which seemed plausible in this day and age and also meant that I would not have to make excuses for having no family nearby.

Soon we were heading out once more into the bright sunshine and Bert guided me to the bandstand. He gave a man a couple of coins and we took our seats in a couple of deck chairs. Bert nodded at a few other people already sitting there and I followed suit.

When we were seated, he leaned over to one of the couples he had acknowledged and said, "lovely to see you again John and Mrs Swayne. This is my good friend Miss Olivia Wylde."

The gentleman said "a pleasure to make your acquaintance, Miss Wylde." I never got to know if his wife was about to speak or not, for at that moment the band started up. I know I keep saying it, but it was just like a film and I loved every minute of their performance.

Children were playing on the grass. Women pushed prams that could have knocked out a small car. Dog walkers kept their dogs securely at their side. Rickety bicycles bumped along the pathways and all the time the brass instruments accompanied them with their music.

I wasn't an expert in brass band music but I did recognise a few of the tracks being played and couldn't help but tap my foot along to the music.

The weather was delightful and a man with a large box attached to his bicycle circulated the band stand audience selling ice cream cones. He only had one flavour, which surprisingly was blackcurrant but it was delicious, rich and creamy. The cone was very sweet, waffle like and harder than I was used to but the effect of the whole thing was perfect. The ice cream seller was doing a roaring trade amongst those seated in the deck chairs and those seated directly on the grass. Soon he had sold out completely and headed off, presumably to stock up once more.

When the band had finished, everyone applauded loudly and slowly the crowd dispersed. Bert held out his hand to help me to stand up and then guided me towards Mr and Mrs Swayne. Bert walked off, chatting with John Swayne while I was left talking to his wife, whose name coincidentally, was Olive.

She pressed me for information about myself, including my family background (which brought about a distinct air of disapproval in her tone) and how I had met Bert. “Oh, we met on the beach.” I replied.

This did nothing to assuage her fears about me based on my lack of family connections. She quite candidly dropped quite a few names into the conservation. Most of whom meant nothing to me apart from a few surnames I recognised but only because they had had streets or businesses named after them locally.

We walked back towards the railway station but instead of joining Mr and Mrs Swayne in entering (they were catching the Totnes train), Bert announced that he needed to head into town to see one of the shopkeepers. The Swaynes looked slightly put out but we all made our goodbyes politely and Bert guided me towards Queens Street.

"I could tell you were not much enamoured of Olive Swayne's company." He declared as we walked down the street. "Therefore, I took the opportunity to make our excuses."
I could have kissed him!

We walked down Queen Street and once more I was enraptured by how everything looked. The variety of shops was astounding, there was a proper ironmongers selling actual metal items, open plan fishmongers and butchers, a book shop, a florist and even Halford's Cycle Co. and Timothy White's which took me back.

We made our way to a tailor's shop and Bert asked me to wait outside. Obviously it was not the done thing for a lady to enter a men's clothing establishment. Directly, he came out carrying a parcel wrapped in brown paper, which he explained contained two pairs of trousers he had ordered a few weeks ago.

He then asked if I would accompany him for luncheon, which I happily agreed to. We made our way down Courtenay Street to the Globe Hotel, where Bert seemed to be well known.

"You come to Newton Abbot regularly then?" I asked while we waited to be seated.

"Oh yes," he replied. "I find it tends to have more up to date fashions than Torquay or Teignmouth and has less tourists."

I smiled. Some things never changed (Newton Abbot was not as touristy as its neighbours) but other things obviously had, imagine Newton Abbot being the more fashionable town!

There was some consternation when we sat down to dine with my declaration of vegetarianism. The hotel, being quite closely located to the livestock market, was famed for its fresh meat dishes but surprisingly the chef offered to create an amazing cheese omelette (luckily I didn't ask for a vegan dish) served with dauphinoise potatoes and fresh vegetables. He later explained to me that he had once cooked for George Bernhard Shaw when working in London and if that gentleman could be vegetarian then he saw no issue with others following suit.

What surprised me most of all, was when the chef explained what he could do for me, Bert insisted on joining me in having the same dish.

"That sounds delicious, I will have the same." He asserted and while his comment was very accurate, I knew he was only doing it to be kind to me. Once more I warmed to this man I had only known for a couple of days.

We talked easily. My lack of knowledge of some aspects of current affairs disappointed him but on other subjects I could converse in detail and even know more than him, largely thanks to my Political Philosophy degree. For example I knew more about Communist Russia than he did. The revolution had only happened a few years earlier and information coming to the UK was sketchy, whereas I had a wealth of information on Lenin and Trotsky. Such as where they had come from, what their ideals were and how they had gained power.

Bert seemed to think that Ramsey MacDonald was cut from the same kind of cloth but I was able to assuage his fear that the Scotsman might help lead to a communist uprising in Britain and that the Labour movement was largely isolating itself from their communist cousins in Europe.

We soon moved from International politics to personal matters.

Bert was quite candid about his life with his wife.

"I loved her. We had been married for twenty years and we hardly ever argued or had a cross word with each other. She felt guilty for us never having children but who knows whose body was the cause of that, it could have been me instead of her. She was sure it was the action of the German measles but we will never know."

I don't think I had met many men who would have suggested that as an option. Not in 2021, let alone 1921. This was an unusual man in so many ways.

He then moved on to his family. "My Grandfather was a builder in Dublin and my Father continued the business after he died. They built a number of properties in some of the nicest parts of Dublin and some I still own today.
My parents could see the writing on the wall and left Dublin just before the last Queen died. We still have properties there but I don't go back any more. The civil war is even worse than the Independence war. Families fighting within themselves and everyone mistrusts everyone else, just in case."

"My parents bought Elm House in 1898 and we all fell in love Lemoncombe and the South Devon countryside. The hills and the sea, the countryside and the woods, were just what we were looking for after the bustle of Dublin. Doris and I took over the house in 1911 when my Father died."

Suddenly he looked at me, "do you know why it is called Lemoncombe?"

I shook my head. "Lemon is an old British name for the elm tree. So Lemoncombe literally means valley of the elms. I fell in love with the elms in the valley and when my parents found that Elm House itself was available, we just had to live there."

I smiled and agreed that I loved the valley too.

The conversation turned to my own circumstances. I explained that I had been born in Newton Abbot but moved away when I was in my twenties to be a nurse but returned in my late twenties. All of this was true. Next came the lies, all of which i had worked out the previous day after my Internet research. I said I had planned to marry a man called John Martin and we got engaged.

“He joined up in 1914 and was sent to the Dardanelles. He never returned.”

I saw the look on Bert's face.

“Oh sorry, I don't mean he died. He just never returned back to England. The last time I saw him was when he sent home on leave but he was quite cold and distant with me. We think he found a Greek woman and he decided that life over there with her was better than life over here with me.”

It was quite a twist on my own real life experiences and I am not quite sure why I made up this story but I felt quite pleased with the final result.

“Have you heard nothing from him since?”

“No, not a word. I don't know if he will ever return and what our situation is. We stopped paying for the house I was living in, so I had to move into an apartment in Teignmouth and pay my own way.”

This last bit was true, just a century out of time.

Bert was naturally sympathetic and I didn't want to dwell too much on John or my white lies but he did ask me more.

“It was a bit of a shock at first, though I haven't seen him since...” I had to work this out “...1917 of course. Who knows where he is or with whom and whether he is still alive.”

“Do you still love him?”

"No, not any more. When he started being cold to me, I felt quite isolated and then when he left me I went into my shell. It was only swimming with my friends which has seen me recover."

I realised that I was telling this man my very personal thoughts. He seemed so easy to talk to and very understanding. I nearly wanted to tell him about coming from 2021 but knew that would be practically impossible, how could he believe me?

CHAPTER THIRTY TWO

After a very pleasant meal, we headed back out into the summer sunshine. We walked along the River Lemon and I wondered whether that was named after the trees too, then cut back through to the station just when the surroundings started to become a bit more industrial.

We hadn't checked train times and there was going to be a bit of a wait before the next train back to Torquay, so we went and sat in the park once more, watching the children playing.

Bert asked, "would it be easier for you to get the train straight back to Teignmouth?"

I panicked. Of course it would be if I was going straight home but I had to swim back through the archway to my home time and car before returning to Teignmouth. What was I to say?

"Erm no, that is fine, I would love to return with you via Torquay. I enjoyed the journey on the way here and it would be lovely to experience that once more."

Bert protested,"I am happy to pay for the ticket if that is the issue?"

"No, but I thank you for the offer."

He did not seem 100% convinced but agreed with what I said. We were a bit more silent on the walk back to the station and while waiting on the platform. Eventually the train came and I was able to wile away the time staring out of the window, feeling very sorry for the lack of trust I was showing this man. Perhaps I would tell him some time.

When we arrived in Torquay, Bert called for another cab and once again it was horse drawn. There were a couple of motorised vehicles but Bert went straight to one of the equine ones. We did talk again on this journey but eventually the conversation turned to what would happen after we had returned to Elm House.

"Would you do me the honour of staying to dinner?"

I would have loved to but I knew I had to be back in the water before 9pm or else I might not be able to see the archway in the dimpsey evening light. What time did they eat dinner in 1921? It was just coming up to 4pm now. Low tide would be at about 8:00pm. My best bet was to refuse and wait out the time on the beach until I could get through the archway, so I decided to refuse.

"I would love to, Bert, but I have to get back to feed my cat, she will be very hungry." This was not true. Even in 2021, I had not had a cat since I had moved to Teignmouth. Our cat had ended up staying with the house!

Bert looked very disappointed and once more I almost felt the need to tell him everything but I resisted.

"Thank you for the offer though, perhaps on another occasion?"

This seemed to make him a little happier. When we had returned to Elm House I thought it best to take my leave of him there and then. "Thank you for a lovely day Bert, I will need to make my way back to Teignmouth now." I said just as the carriage arrived into the driveway.

"I will arrange for the carriage to take you home." he declared and despite my protestations he leaned forward to speak to the driver and pressed some money into his hand, pointing back towards me. I wasn't quite sure what to do.

Bert took my hand, kissed it and said "the pleasure has been all mine Miss Wylde and I look forward to the next occasion when I get to enjoy your company."

He nodded at me and then the carriage driver, who then took the hint and we started. I waited until the carriage had got out of eyeline and ear shot, just in case and called to the driver to come to a halt.

"It is alright driver, you can drop me here. I plan to see some friends." He looked a bit perturbed until I added. "You can keep the money that Mr Windyett gave to you."

This made him very happy as he would earn the money without having to travel to Teignmouth and back.

After I had alighted, I made my way surreptitiously back down the lane, keeping an eye out for Bert on the way but there seemed to be no one around. Despite this, I still got into a bit of a run when I passed the entrance way to Elm House Drive and didn't stop until I had reached the steps to the cove.
I could see that the archway was not anywhere near visible yet, as the tide was too high. I made my way down to the beach and headed to my little hiding place with my dry bag and swimming costume. Everything was still there, which was good news.

I found a suitable spot to sit and wait for the tide. I wished I had brought my Kindle with me but also wondered whether it would work back in time, did you read the books online (and of course there would be no internet for another 70 years or so) or did you download them to your kindle? I wasn't quite sure.

The time passed slowly and the sea height seemed to drop even more slowly. It was not until 6:30pm that I saw the first bits of the archway start to appear. It was lucky that at just that moment I looked around the cove and spotted Bert walking down the steps towards the beach. Fortunately he hadn't spotted me yet and I was able to hide behind some of the rocks.

He went and sat in the same place where he was sitting on the day we first met. Oh no, what was I to do now? A half hour later he was still there and the water level was dropping. Now I could see about a couple of feet gap below the archway. Still Bert sat there. I decided to get changed into my swimming gear so that I would be ready if and when he went again. 8 o'clock came and still Bert was there. I started to panic. What would happen if I was unable to get back? Where would I sleep? Would I ever be able to get back again? Might it only work on the same day?

Eventually at about 8:15 pm Bert started to make his way back up the steps. I waited patiently for him to disappear and then ran into the sea and started to swim towards the archway. By the time I had reached the archway, you could tell that the water level was just beginning to rise again but I could still swim through.

When I turned around again, I was once more presented with two archways and made my way through the left hand one, back into the morning gloom of 2021. I was absolutely exhausted, as I had swum much more quickly than I would do normally. So the journey back to the beach was actually quite hard work but the adrenalin of nearly getting stuck in the past gave me enough energy to return to shore.

I almost staggered out of the water and a few people watched me cautiously but I ignored them and went and sat down on some of the rocks. After a while I recovered and got changed. Once more I was struck by a feeling of anti-climax after returning to my own time. Somehow when I was back in 1921 with Bert, everything seemed more vibrant. But was it real?
I wasn't quite sure what was going on and how it would all end. However one thing I did know, I wanted to return to Bert and

1921 again and soon.

CHAPTER THIRTY THREE

29th May 2021 – Teignmouth

The next day I was unable to swim in the morning, as I had a couple of client appointments and the day after that was the online networking meeting that I had recently been invited to and promised that I would attend, so that day was out too. Though I did consider missing the meeting and heading off to Lemoncombe anyway but I would be letting down the financial advisor who had kindly invited me.

There was also a little part of me which did not want to appear too keen to return and see Bert again. I no longer had the excuse of the clothes to return, what would I give for my reason for seeing him this time. This did perturb me somewhat.

I was already a bit grumpy as my massage bed had broken after one of my client appointments, so that meant I had to cancel some appointments while I waited for a new bed to arrive. So I had reduced income and I also had to spend money buying a new bed. I was therefore really looking forward to heading back to 1921 to take my mind off things.

Therefore I headed back to Lemoncombe Beach once more on a couple of days later. Low tide was going to be at about 10:30am, so when I arrived I was surprised to realise that I could see no sign of the archway at 9:30am. I got changed but still at 9:45am there was no sign. I double checked the tide times on my phone and it confirmed that low tide was due at around 10:30am. I waited until 10:15am and decided to swim out. When I reached the place where the archway was, there was still no sign of it above water. Remembering what little I knew about tides, I recalled that the height of the high and low tides did vary and I realised that the tide was not going to be low enough today. If that was the case today, would it be the same on other days, if so, what was I to do?

Perhaps if I dived underwater I would be able to swim through the archway. However, there were two problems with this. Firstly I was not 100% sure where exactly the archway was and if I was slightly off target I would just be swimming into rocks. Secondly I was frightened by the idea, and some sort of claustrophobia started to kick in. There was also the possibility that the archway would not work underwater. Who knew how these time portals existed and whether water got in the way or not?

I gave up and swam disconsolately back to the beach once more. With a very disappointed feeling I got changed back into my clothes. I realised how much I was looking forward to seeing Bert again after a couple of days of not enjoying his company.

Now I was presented with another possibility which shook me even more than I expected it to. What would happen if I was never to see him again?

Just the thought of it made my stomach drop. That was not something I even wanted to think about.

I headed home and checked the tide times and heights for the next week or two at Lemoncombe. I knew today was not low enough but two days ago it was, just about. I could see that the previous few days had been particularly low tides and there were only going to be a couple of days in about 10 days time when the tides would be low enough to possibly let me through. The only problem would be that the low tides would be at about 2pm in the afternoon. This would be fine for me heading back in time but I wouldn't be able to go there and back in the same day, unless I worked out some way of swimming through the archway at night. Perhaps there would be a full moon?

I checked and there wouldn't be. Then I realised I would have to check the full moon dates for 1921. Incredibly these were available online and I was able to see that there was a full moon on the right date in June in 1921 which would work perfectly.

Perhaps I could do it?
What would happen if it was cloudy or raining?
Perhaps I could sleep overnight somewhere and return the next afternoon?

I spent the next few days worrying about all these things in my mind. I also needed to try and determine what I was going to do workwise.

The new bed would take some time to arrive and while some people waited patiently for me to get my new massage bed but as time dragged on, many went elsewhere. I couldn't do treatments at Suze's place as there wasn't a spare room and anyway she worked from home herself.

This all left me homeless, loveless and without much income. Life was looking a bit shit, so a visit to 1921 seemed very enticing.

I decided to make it work, one way or another.

CHAPTER THIRTY FOUR

10th June 1921 - Lemoncombe Beach

Bert was sitting on the rocks once more. This time he knew exactly what he was waiting for but he was beginning to think that it would not happen again.

Miss Wylde had swam ashore at this very beach two weeks ago. She had then returned to him one day later. On both days they had spent a very pleasant time together and he wanted to see her again. Hence his reason for returning to the beach where he had first encountered her.

He had been here for ten days in a row but without success. He was beginning to feel that his time was wasted and that she would never return.

Once more the day passed with no success. It was different from his first period of waiting. This time, every day hurt more than the previous day.

CHAPTER THIRTY FIVE

11th June 2021 - Lemoncombe Beach

Annoyingly, the wind picked up heavily on the 10th June and the waves at Lemoncombe were quite severe, so I decided not to risk the swim. I headed back on the 11th and it was a totally different day. The sky was clear, there was no wind and the sea was so calm. The beach was much busier than other days we had been to Lemoncombe, as it was a warm early summer day and I had arrived there much later than before.

I got changed on the beach and put my 1921 things into the dry bag, as I had before. I then headed out into the busy sea. As it was low tide, there were quite a few children playing in the shallows with their inflatables, plus there were older children and adults heading out on paddle boards, which seemed to have multiplied wildly during lockdown.

I managed to dodge all of these people and headed out towards the archway which was just about visible this time, obviously the tide was low but not quite as low as two weeks previously. The only problem was that a few paddle boarders had also decided to head that way and decided to take a break quite close to the archway itself.

I couldn't head under the archway without them seeing. Would it matter?

Would someone try to follow me or worry if I was ok or not?

I would have preferred to do this without anyone seeing but I couldn't wait indefinitely. I nodded hello to a couple of them and then swam in circles for a minute or two. One of them looked like they were getting ready to get moving again.

Eventually all but one of them had gone, and the one who was left was just sitting on his board, playing with his mobile phone. I could see the archway was there but not as much of a gap as I would like and every passing minute was making it smaller. *Go on, bugger off*, I thought to myself. Then berated myself for being a bit rude!

Finally, he finished with his phone, realised that his friends had gone and so he packed his phone away in his dry bag and paddled off to follow them.

The archway was before me once more and I looked around but no one was watching me now. Knowing that I had limited time, I started to head towards it once more. For some reason, I felt more trepidation than I had the last time. I was not sure what reaction I would find from Bert on the other side, as I had been away for nigh on ten days. Plus of course there was the very good chance that I wouldn't be able to get back at all.

Taking a deep breath, even though I didn't need to go underwater, I swam through the archway holding my breath all the way!

The sun was in a different position to the other times I had swum around and was actually shining down to my right. This made it easier to acclimatise to my situation when I got through the archway. I turned around and there were the two archways in front of me once more.

I didn't hesitate and swam straight through the right hand arch. On getting through, I was pleased to see that it was sunny on this side as well. For the first time I could see other swimmers in the sea in 1921.

It was now June after all, but it still caught me off guard. The tide was low here too, so it didn't take me long to swim to shore. I planned on getting changed in my usual spot on the rocks but I spotted Bert sitting where I had first encountered him. This caught me off guard for a moment. I hadn't thought he would be here again but of course he said he often came down to the beach and it was mid afternoon, so a perfect time for him to be here.

For the first time he wasn't wearing trousers but what appeared to be three quarter length pants, tucked into his tartan socks. Also, despite the warm day, he had a matching tartan tank top over his white shirt and tie. This would be very formal in 2021 but I felt it was probably quite casual attire for Bert.

“Miss Wylde, I see you have been swimming again. I did not see you enter the water, I must have missed it despite the fact I have been sitting here for over an hour.”

“Umm, I swam around from the other cove.”

I pointed over my shoulder towards the archway.

“I did not know there was any way you could reach that cove on foot.” replied Bert.

“Oh I swam through the archway earlier and have just returned now.”

Quickly changing the subject I said, “would you mind if I got changed now?”

Bert flushed a bit which I found quite endearing and then politely got up and walked back towards the steps. As it was quite warm and dry, my changing was quick and easy. Soon I was dressed in a long summer dress which I estimated was suitably demure for 1921 and I called back to Bert, who appeared to be investigating some interesting rocks.

“It's okay, you can look again now.” He turned back to look at me and I was pleased to see a smile cross his face. I had obviously chosen well.

Then my orange dry bag caught his eye. “That bag is very brightly coloured.”

“Yes,”I said, “it is to help me to be seen when I am swimming.”

“If I may?” He enquired and when I nodded, he leaned forward and took hold of it. Feeling the texture and the weight, then taking particular interest in the way the bag folded over to seal itself. “I assume it is waterproof and airtight then?”

I was slightly flummoxed by this interest in what was only a bag but then realised much of this technology was decades in the future and therefore it would be rather extraordinary to someone like Bert.

“Yes, it is very useful for longer swims, such as today, as you can safely take your things around with you. I got it from...ummm... America.”

I had thought my American explanation would work, as they might be seen as a source of all things modern in this time but he looked at me somewhat quizzically. Of course without the Internet and other global communication systems, there would be no easy way of finding things from other countries in the 1920s. Then something popped into my head.

“I ordered from a mail order catalogue.”

He nodded and said, “oh, very good.” Thankfully that seemed to have worked.

“Did your swimming costume come from a similar source? I have not seen anything quite like that before.”

“Yes.” I replied, but wanting to get off the subject of things that I should really not have in the 1920s, I decided to steer the conversation in another direction.

“So how long have you been sitting here today Bert?”

He seemed to be taken slightly off guard by the change in direction but quickly re-adjusted and said, "I have been coming down here in the mornings to sit and look at the sea. I used to come down with Doris and we would watch the boats go by and the various birds. Doris always liked watching the birds."

Suddenly he looked very sad and drawn but then he looked at me once more and smiled.

"You are nothing like Doris," he said.

I was not sure what to say in response to this, so he continued.

"She would never have swum so far, or run her own business, or talked to a strange man on the beach."

I still was unsure what to say and whether I had misjudged how to handle such things in the 1920s. He noticed my discomfort and so continued once more.

"But I like that about you. I loved Doris, but I do wish some women would not be so controlled by the men in their lives. This is the 1920s after all. The modern age is upon us and things are changing. You, Miss Wylde, are one of the new types of women and I applaud you for that."

This man was very special to think and say such things. If only he knew what was to come, I wonder whether he would be so full of praise for change.

I found myself beginning to realise something that had only partially crossed my mind so far. I could spend more time with this man quite happily and could possibly contemplate him as a life partner.

But could that happen? I was from 2021, he was from 1921. Forgetting all the things about a paradox being created or me becoming my own grandmother, could I actually live in 1921 and would he actually want me to?

We had a connection, that was obvious, but we didn't really know each other that well and apart from a couple of brief visits, I had no idea what it was like living in the 1920s.

My life in 2021 was pretty shit but could I, or would I, risk what little I had back then for a new life here?

I told myself to be sensible, take my time and not to rush into anything stupid.

All of this had taken milliseconds to consider but Bert was still waiting for me to reply to his earlier comment.

"Thank you Bert, I will take that as a complement and I wholeheartedly agree, women's lives can only change for the better in the coming years."

Once more he nodded.

"Did you have plans for today, or would like to spend some more time in my company?"

I could have kissed him but I knew that would not be the done thing and also I did not know how he would react.

"I have no immediate plans. So that would be very pleasurable Bert," I answered demurely.

We spent the rest of the afternoon walking through the woods around Lemoncombe. The elm trees, which would be later wiped out by Dutch elm disease, were very prolific in the area, hence the name of the valley. All in all it was a very pleasant afternoon. Bert had taken my bag and dropped it off at the house, before we left from a back gate. He brought with him two bottles of water with rubber stoppers in them and we would stop periodically to regain our breath and quench our thirst. The views from the gaps in the trees were majestic looking out towards Torbay or the other way towards the Teign estuary.

The best thing about the walk though was Bert's attention to me.

I am a fairly modern girl but having an attentive man, worried about my comfort and concerns was actually a big relief after the inattention shown to me by John.

Bert was a good old fashioned gentleman and he genuinely seemed to care and be concerned for my welfare, rather than just out of some strange duty or honour.

We returned to the house at about 4pm and Mrs Holmes had provided afternoon tea for us. I laughed when both Bert and I added our clotted cream (apparently made from Bert's own dairy) first to the scones.

“At least you do it the proper Devon way.” I laughed.

“I am sorry, what do you mean?” he looked at me, puzzled.

“You put the cream on first and then the jam. That is the Devon way, the Cornish put on the jam first.”

“Do they? Why would they do that? You wouldn’t put on the butter after the jam would you?” he asked.

“No, of course not. But in my time the Cornish tell us their way is right and the Devonshire folk say theirs is the right way. It could lead to a war.” I laughed.

“Such things are not to be taken lightly and what do you mean by saying in your time?”

I doubly cursed myself. One for the slip about “my time” and secondly for forgetting they had just come out of a terrible war and people didn't joke about such things here.

“Sorry I did not mean offence and I meant that in my time I have heard people talking about it.”

Thankfully he did not pursue the matter and I promised myself that I needed to be more careful with what I said or mentioned.

CHAPTER THIRTY SIX

11th June 1921 – Lemoncombe

Once again the time with Bert seemed to fly by. This time it was already afternoon by the time that I first arrived in 1921, so we would not have the whole day to spend together anyway.

As the evening drew in, he invited me to dinner, which I accepted with relish. Once more we chatted about many things and then he raised the question of my returning home.

I could tell he had been wrestling with different ideas in his head during dinner and he finally seemed to make a decision and raise the issue.

"Miss Wylde, I am not happy for a lady to travel alone in a carriage on the road back to Teignmouth at night. I know it is not the done thing for a single lady to share a house with a widowed man but the spare room is already made up, no-one but the people in this house would be aware and I would be much happier to know you are safe and warm here, rather than risking a journey back on that road."

He almost sighed with relief when he finished the rather long sentence.

I almost could have cried with happiness at the offer. This was perfect for me. I would not have to return to the future in the veil of moonlight or if that were not possible, kip down somewhere outside overnight. This would enable me to get a good night's sleep, spend some more time with Bert and then swim back in the daylight at low tide tomorrow.

I had to admit the bit about spending more time with Bert was the most satisfying element of the arrangement. I had found every moment with him enjoyable and it just meant I wanted to spend more and more time with him. My answer was therefore easy to give to him.

“That is very kind Bert. If it is really no trouble then I would be delighted to accept your offer.”

This time you could practically see him expand with happiness. A large smile also played on his face as he said “Excellent. Are you proficient in the game of cribbage? Perhaps we could play a round or two after dinner?”

I nodded and smiled.

We did indeed play cribbage. I needed to be refreshed of the rules, as I hadn't played for many years but soon got back into the habit of “fifteen two, fifteen four...” and had another lovely evening.

It was the first time I had spent time in the drawing room, a room which was obviously only used by Bert in the evening. 9:30pm arrived and Bert announced that it was time for bed. He very kindly showed me towards my room but made no attempt to come towards the doorway, let alone enter the room, so I said my thanks and went to bed.

At some point someone must have placed a bowl of now tepid water in the room, together with a towel and flannel. There was also something I was dreading using – the chamber pot.

During the day when I had needed to go I had nipped behind a bush to go. When I had raised the matter in the evening with Bert, he had blushed and directed me towards the outside privy with a gaslight in my hand. As I had got close to it and the aroma had hit me, I had quickly decided to dart into a bush and go for a wee.

Tonight was a different matter altogether. I needed to go for the second option on the list of lavatory choices and this meant sitting on a large potty and then hiding it away from myself for the night.

There was nothing for it, it had to be done, so I did it,making sure I knew where the toilet paper was before I started. Actually the process was easier than I had expected, the only problem was that the loo paper was a bit like the stuff we used to have at school which was more likely to spread the residue rather than absorb it.

Within a few minutes I was done. The pot was in a corner festering under a cloth which had come with it. I washed my hands and face and retired to bed. I was wearing just a t-shirt that I had left in my bag as the best alternative to nightwear. The bed was lumpier than I was used to and the bedding was much heavier than we would have in the 21st Century but I would later be grateful for that when the night got colder.

I actually slept surprisingly well and in the morning I could just about tell that the sun was shining through the heavy curtains. I looked into the corner of the room and could see that someone must have come into the room and taken the chamber pot. I pitied the poor chamber maid whose job that was. Bert only had a few servants and young Lily was left with most of the less savoury tasks.

I washed again and had no alternative but to wear the same clothing as the day before. Fortunately I had the presence of mind to include a hairbrush and body spray in my dry bag, so I could at least make myself a bit more agreeable in presentation.

Feeling that I had looked worse on some mornings, I headed downstairs to find out what my next options were. I found Bert already up and breakfasting in the dining room.

He directed me to the little self service area, suggesting I should ask if there was anything else I wanted and therefore I helped myself to the eggs, tomatoes, mushrooms and toast. What I would have done for a bit of brown sauce but that wasn't on offer. To be honest I probably would have preferred yoghurt and granola but I wasn't so stupid as to ask for anything like that.

Bert asked after my sleeping arrangements and my general health this morning and we had another easy and pleasant chat. He then suggested that we take a trip that morning to Torquay to collect some paperwork from his attorney.

I said that I would be delighted and would my attire be satisfactory for the occasion. He said that it would be perfectly acceptable but perhaps, while he was meeting his attorney I could visit the local department store and find myself some fresh clothing for the day, he had an account there so it would be no problem.

An hour later I felt a bit like Julia Roberts in Pretty Woman, while a middle aged woman took my measurements and placed a number of under and over garments on a chair for me to put on. She even found me a suitable hat.

When I left the store I was wearing new 1921 clothes and also carrying a couple of boxes for evening and lounge wear. I was normally a very independent woman but the past few months had knocked me badly and Bert did seem inclined to spoil me, so why not let him?

CHAPTER THIRTY SEVEN

We met once more in the main street which was looking much cleaner and more refined in 1921 despite having a number of vehicles travelling up and down it, pumping out fumes or dropping horse manure.

Bert had arranged for the groom to meet me at the store and collect my boxes and then pick him up from his attorney. We then headed to the Pavilion, which I now learned was a theatre in 1921 but it also had lounge bars and cafés and we headed there for some lunch in one of the oak panelled rooms.

Once more, I felt like I was being wined and dined in a film. A maitre d' took our order and barely a muscle moved in his face when I explained that I was a vegetarian. His smile never wavered as he asked, "does madam eat fish?"

I almost replied apologetically, "no, sorry."

"It is not a problem madam, how about eggs and cheese?"

It was my turn to smile when I said "Oh yes, everything but meat and fish."

Bert then added, "I will join the lady in her vegetarian diet and share food with her."

"Excellent Mr Windyett, I will speak to the kitchen and we will bring you a series of dishes."

"Thank you, that is very kind."

"It is not a problem Madam, we recently had a party of Hindus from India who also do not eat meat and we were able to cater for them for a week, though we did have to get in some extra spices as they found the English food somewhat bland."

He looked at us both conspiratorially, "I can quite understand as I served under the Governor of Penang for fifteen years."

I smiled and said, "well I do like Indian food myself."

Bert looked at me with mild surprise at this declaration.

The maitre d' nodded and said, "I will mention this to the kitchen."

We were brought a lovely white wine to go with our soup starter. The soup was onion and tasted delicious.

We were then brought a series of small dishes that the kitchen had prepared for us. Including peppered grilled tomatoes, spinach omelette, turmeric potatoes and blue cheese vol au vents.

Our fellow diners looked at our food with a mixture of envy, confusion and haughtiness. Bert and I looked on with hunger and were just happy to get started.

The food was delicious and we said as much when the maitre d' checked on us to make sure everything was to our satisfaction. We managed to polish it all off and afterwards Bert said, "I think I could quite happily become vegetarian if we are to be treated like this every day."

I laughed, "I am happy to continue to try and convert you Bert."

This comment made him stop and look at me for a while. Our gazes met, after a moment I looked away demurely and I wondered why he was looking at me so intently.

After lunch we left the Pavilion and decided to walk along the harbour side. So far I had been blessed to only visit 1921 on reasonably good days, and I wondered what it would be like on a squally, rainy day. Also I was not stupid. I knew that these were the years before the welfare state and a lot of simple sanitation. There would be poverty, illness and hardship all around me.

Just for a moment though, I allowed myself to enjoy this idyllic "Merchant Ivory-esque" world, because a girl needs to have some pleasure sometimes. In fact as we walked along the seafront in the direction of Paignton, there were as many (if not more) poor and destitute people as there were people of the smart and middle classes.

The main difference seemed to be what they were doing. This was a Saturday and, I later found out, that most working people worked on Saturdays, at least until mid afternoon. Whereas the professionals and middle classes were more likely to be free for leisure activities.

A group of dirt-covered workmen carrying spades had obviously just finished work for the week as they were all carrying and drinking bottles of beer. Other men were busy pushing carts full of everything you could imagine. Plus there were a few vagrants sitting and mumbling to themselves.

Interspersed with this were couples walking arm in arm in the June sunshine. Well dressed young ladies (presumably nannies or maids) pushing industrial looking prams containing the pampered offspring of some well off and absent parents.

Into this mix came Bert and myself. We walked separately, I still wasn't aware of what the etiquette should be and I wasn't going to make a fool of myself and initiate anything. We chatted amiably. Of course my knowledge of current affairs was limited, which didn't surprise Bert too much as women probably weren't supposed to be that up to speed in 1921.

Every now and then I did surprise him though with my wider knowledge. There was a man selling newspaper broadsheets from a small booth. I was fascinated to learn how people reported the events of the time and so I bounded over in a most un-ladylike fashion to pick up a copy. Then I realised that I had no money on me but Bert came to my rescue paying the fee to the man.

I opened the paper to see that it was the “Torbay Express and South Devon Echo”, presumably some precursor to the later “Herald Express” that I had known. We took the paper to one of the benches and read it together. I was as fascinated by the adverts as I was with the actual news articles.

I almost laughed to see an advert for one of the enormous “Perambulators” along with such staples as coal tar soap and Bourneville Cocoa.

As well as local news the paper carried wider stories and Bert pointed out a story about some Royal Irish Constabulary officers being murdered in Co. Mayo in Ireland. Bert, of course, had grown up and lived in Dublin and he said, “Ireland is a tinderbox waiting to happen.”
I nodded and said, “even if we pull out completely, they will fight each other as there are just too many different opinions. With people like Michael Collins and Eamon de Valeira supposedly on the same side but hating each other, it will not end easily. Plus you have the Catholics in Ulster who will never be happy to be part of the United Kingdom.”

I looked at him and realised that once more I had spoken too much. I had studied early twentieth century history at University (in modules about political philosophy) and knew that 1921 and 1922 were crunch years for the Republic and the Union.

I thought quickly and said, “I have some distant relatives in

Enniskillen, who sometimes write about it."

He looked at me with that look that I would later come to recognise to mean "are you sure?" but he seemed to let it pass. I quickly changed the subject by pointing out the advert for cocoa.

The rest of the afternoon went by easily. The sun was out and the air was clearer than I expected. I am sure that if I had been in one of the larger cities or one of the Northern mill towns, things would be very different but down there on the English Riviera the sun was out, the sky was blue and everything looked gorgeous.

We walked back towards Torquay once more and after I stumbled slightly in my new shoes, Bert held out his arm to steady me. After I had regained my balance, we kept our arms together and walked with our arms entwined. A little thrill went down my back. What was I doing? I was acting like a little girl! Oh to hell with it, why not for a change!

Bert bought us both ice creams, which were absolutely delicious and we continued to chat easily and I made sure I steered clear of politics. We got back to the horse and carriage, which was waiting for us by the harbour and Bert held out his hand once more to help me up before sitting down beside me.

I felt like a princess in a fairy carriage but the moment was quickly spoiled by a swooping gull which took a swipe at my ice cream. I spilled my ice cream into Bert's lap and he jumped up at the feel of the cold on his nether regions and threw his own ice cream at the gull who was still pestering us. The gull and a few of its companions then flew off to where Bert's ice cream had landed having managed a little victory.

I looked down at the ice cream in Bert's lap, which he was now shovelling onto the pavement and I couldn't stop myself from laughing. He looked at me in distress and then horror. When he started to shake I wondered whether I had gone too far but then the shake turned into him breaking down in howls of laughter. The groom looked at Bert with some confusion as he passed him a cloth to clean up the mess. Bert and I continued to laugh through the tears that were now brimming in both of our eyes.

I realised that this had been a very special and defining day. I had missed the low tide this afternoon and I was wondering whether I wanted to try and use the moonlight later tonight or not. But when Bert invited me to dinner once more and asked if I wished to stay again that evening I acquiesced rather more quickly than I expected to.

CHAPTER THIRTY EIGHT

My plan was to stay one more night, spend some time with Bert in the morning and head back to 2021 in the afternoon. After that I was unsure what my new plans would be. I knew that the low tide would be at around 3pm that afternoon, so I planned to get to the beach by 2pm in order to ensure that I would have the longest possible time to get back home.

Bert seemed occupied at breakfast. A number of times he said something like "Miss Wylde I wonder if..." but then stopped himself and either went silent or went off on a tangent. I wasn't quite sure what was on his mind and was slightly concerned that he was going to ask me to join him somewhere that afternoon.

I explained that I had plans that afternoon so would need to be away from around 1:30pm. Therefore we went for a short coastal walk in the morning, enjoying the views back over towards Teignmouth and Dawlish, the red rocks glowing in the June morning sunshine.

We passed more people today out walking as it was a Sunday and everyone would be enjoying their day of rest, after visiting church. No rushing to the supermarket or garden centres in 1921!

Mrs Holmes then prepared us a light lunch that we ate outside on the terrace. The air was lovely and warm for June and early summer smells from the garden made it quite idyllic. The only matter which slightly spoiled it was that Mrs Holmes had made half of the sandwiches with cold ham, either forgetting or choosing to forget that I was vegetarian. I didn't make a meal of it, but Bert was very apologetic. He said, “I am sure she just forgot, over time she will learn to remember that you are vegetarian and not to serve such things.”

After he said this, he held his hand up to his mouth as if he had said too much but I was confused by this action. Once more he seemed preoccupied, as if he had something important to say but could not bring himself to mention it. So we spent a slightly uneasy last half hour sitting on the terrace taking in the sunshine.

Despite all of that, it was with much heaviness of heart that I took my leave of Bert. There were still a number of confusing matters to sort out. Firstly he wanted to arrange a carriage to take me back to Teignmouth but I said that I had some people picking me up from the main road. Then he wanted to accompany me to make sure I was safe. I thanked him but said that would not be necessary.

Then came the matter of my clothes and shoes that he had bought for me the day before. There was no way I could carry them back with me to 2021. The only thing I could think of was to ask Bert to look after them for me, until I returned another day. At first he seemed not sure about this but then he suddenly seemed happy and agreed.

Once more he seemed to have something on his mind. “Miss Wylde...” He started, but then trailed off.

I wondered whether he was going to offer to drive me back to Teignmouth himself or something similar and waited. But once more he stumbled and said “Ummm.... errr, have a safe journey back to Teignmouth and return to me again soon.”

I thanked him and left.

I had already planned my route. I could walk up the lane and then join the footpath further up and do a loop through the fields which took me another way around to the lower path which headed down to the beach. This way I could avoid any prying eyes wondering where I was heading.

This passed without any issues and I got to the beach just before 2pm. Walking down the steps I looked out and couldn't see the archway yet but I knew there was still another hour to go, so carried on down to the beach itself.

With it being a warm sunny Sunday in June, the beach was the busiest I had yet seen it. I began to realise how different my swimming costume must seem to Bert. The ladies seemed to be draped from head to toe in over the top swimming costumes. Bizarrely though, although some men were also heavily attired, some were wearing short trunks that did not leave much to the imagination. I quickly looked away and found a quieter spot near some of the rocks.

I decided to wait a little longer for the archway to start to appear before heading into the water, as I didn't want to tread water or get too wrinkly. However, after waiting for twenty minutes, there was still no sign of the archway. I decided to get changed, thinking that it might be one of those times when you need to do something to make something else happen rather than just wait for it. I knew there was no logic in this thinking but it was a nice day to have a swim anyway, so why not enjoy it?

When I had gotten changed into my swimming costume and put my clothes and shoes into the bright orange dry bag, I received some strange glances from my fellow beach residents. I was not sure whether this was a result of my (relatively) revealing swimming costume or the strangeness of my bright orange bag, or maybe a combination of the two. Oh well, I would soon be out of their hair.

I was disconcerted to see that the archway was still not visible and time was beginning to march onwards. It was now 2:30pm and low tide was due for 2:58pm to be precise. Hell. What was I going to do if the tide was not low enough. I had already decided not to risk trying to swim underwater to get through it and I had no idea how long it would be until the next tide low enough for the archway to appear.

At 2:40pm I decided I had to go for it and started to swim out. Heading straight towards the place where I knew the archway to be, hoping that it would suddenly appear. However I knew that this was very unlikely to happen. I reached the spot where I had encountered the paddle boarder just a couple of days earlier in my timeline and a hundred years in the future in everyone else's.

No luck, the archway did not appear. I swam around and around but no, nothing. Could i swim under the water and get through? I didn't think so. Firstly I was not 100% sure where exactly the archway was. Secondly how deep I would have to swim to locate it and thirdly my tow float would make swimming under water more difficult as it would drag me back to the surface.

I couldn't believe that for the second time I had been defeated by the elements. I did something that I had never done before in my life, I smacked the water with my hand, for all the good it did. Eventually I gave up, turned tail and headed back towards the beach.

I was absolutely dejected. What was I going to do?

I was stranded in 1921 until there was another low tide. I know Bert was just up the road but I had just left him to go and spend time in Teignmouth. I couldn't waltz back up and say “Oh sorry I've changed my mind and decided to come back after all.”

But what were my options?

Based on my analysis from before, the next time there would be a low enough tide to get through the archway would be in a couple of week's time. How was I to survive in 1921 until that time?

Even if I went back to Bert's he would think it very odd after more than a couple of days. So where else could I go?

Of course I had relatives back in 1921 but there were three problems with that.
1 – I wasn't 100% sure where they lived
2 – my great grandmother on one side was bringing up my grandmother and three of her siblings all by herself, as my great grandfather had died young, so the last thing she would want would be another mouth to feed. My other great grandparents were unknown to me, as my grandfather was placed into care at a young age and never knew them. He would only be about 10 years old right now.
3 – even if any of my relatives could support me, could you imagine the conversation we would have? "Hello I'm your descendent from the future, I came back in time by swimming through an archway in the sea but now I'm stranded here and I was wondering whether you could put me up for a while. Why are you screaming? No, wait! Don't try to get a policeman!"

Yes, exactly. Not the best option.

Was there anyone else I could go to for support?

Were there charities in 1921 that would support someone like me?

What was someone like me?

I'm not sure I could explain my predicament without getting locked up in a mental asylum, as I think such establishments were named in this inter-war period.

All this was running through my brain, while I got changed on the beach once more. The other beach patrons seemed to have moved on from being horrified by my appearance now and chose just to ignore me instead. That suited me fine as it gave me time to mull over my own thoughts.

Talking about my thoughts, they kept bouncing back to thinking about Bert, which wasn't helping. I know he had been kind to me but there was so much more about him. He was gentle, he really seemed to care about what I thought and did and every time we chatted it was so easy, like we had been chatting together for all our lives.

As I left the beach I was thinking about him again and wondering if there was any way I could approach him to help me in my current predicament, even if only for a short time. Once more his face popped into my thoughts and the way we laughed after the ice cream had dropped into his private parts brought a large smile to my face.

So deep in thought was I while I walked up the steps, that I failed to notice the person walking down the steps, who was also not looking where they were going and was also deep in thought.

We both looked up and into each other's eyes. "Miss Wylde!" "Bert!" we exclaimed in unison. "I was just thinking about you." We both said.

Once more a look of anguish seemed to cross Bert's face but this time he seemed to come to some kind of decision.

A big smile crossed his face and it made him look even more handsome than ever.

"Miss Wylde..." again he hesitated but this time he did continue. "Miss Wylde, would you do me the honour of consenting to be my wife?"

I stumbled in shock and nearly fell back down the steps but just in time, Bert held out his hand to stop me and brought me level once more.

I replied with the most surety than I ever had in my life. “Yes Bert, I would love to be your wife!”.

The big smile that now crossed his face almost made me melt and despite myself, the etiquette and whatever else I was doing wrong, I leaned forward, gave him a big kiss directly on the lips and then followed it up with a massive hug!

CHAPTER THIRTY NINE

Of course what I should really write about next was that everything after that went swimmingly and they all "lived happily ever after". Well, part of that was true but I needed to get through a lot of little hiccoughs first.

The first thing I had to deal with was the fact that I had no home, no possessions and no friends or family in 1921. In reality it would probably have been better at this point to tell Bert the truth, but of course I did not think he would ever believe me and it was one hell of a story to try and tell.

However the back story I had to create to cover the various ambiguities in my life ended up being even more convoluted and hard to maintain. At first the bit about me being an orphan was perfect to cover why I had no family but apart from that, where did I live, where were my clothes? How did I support myself and where were my friends?

In the end I came up with a story about a violent man who had dominated me for years and eventually I managed to escape him to come to Lemoncombe. When I had returned to him he had incarcerated me until I had managed to escape just two days ago and come back to Lemoncombe again.

I never wanted to return, so that chapter in my life was now over and I looked forward to my new chapter. Bert had clung to me at this point and I burst into tears. They were tears of sadness from me for lying to this lovely man but tears of joy for the warm feeling of being in his arms.

There was nothing to stop us getting married now and to save time of having the banns read out, we went to the registry office in Newton Abbot with just Mr and Mrs Holmes as our witnesses.

So began the next part of my life journey. Did I ever consider returning to 2021 in those early days? No, not really. I knew some of my friends would miss me but not enough to justify worrying too much. My life imprint back there was much more minimal than it should have been, plus I was at a real low both psychologically and financially, whereas here I had an opportunity for true happiness.

Some things were easier than I would have thought possible. If I had just appeared in 2021, I would find it very hard to do anything because I would not exist on any official records. I would have no NI number, no history of schooling or work, no birth registration.

When we went to the registry office, I said that I had no birth certificate because I was an orphan and, despite a little consternation at first, they said "that kind of things is happening all the time, no problem" and that was that. Coincidentally just two weeks after Bert proposed to me, the 1921 census was carried out and I then started to exist officially on the records, though it did take me a little while to work out what my birth year should be!

One issue that also arose on the census was my profession. It was not unusual for many women in the 1920s to not have a profession but I was not going to be the doting housewife and therefore I needed to find a new role in life.

I didn't think that 1921 was ready for the Bowen Therapy yet and even though I could have set up doing chiropracty or physiotherapy, I didn't believe that the world was ready for female practitioners yet. I did consider nursing, as I had done basic training before going into bodywork. But I did think that my knowledge would probably be totally out of sync with the common practices in 1921.

So what could I do?

The answer came about by accident. A few days after our marriage, I was at home in our house (I hadn't yet got bored about thinking about it as "our house") when Bert's new estate manager had called to see Bert with an urgent problem.

Unfortunately Bert wasn't there and we couldn't get hold of him, one thing I did miss was the ease of using mobile phones to get hold of someone.

Robin, the estate manager, wanted to know whether to order some new fertiliser, as the supplier only had a small amount left and if we didn't buy it today they would sell it to someone else. He had been trying to get hold of Bert but with the marriage and following time off, Bert had not got back to him.

I talked it through with Robin, and he explained how important this particular fertiliser was to the clay-rich soils on which our farms stood. If we didn't secure this fertiliser today, our yields in the autumn would not be as high. Having heard all the details, I took the executive decision of letting Robin know he could go ahead and buy the fertiliser and I would take the responsibility with Mr Windyett.

Robin was at first unsure but when I assured him that he would not be blamed for anything, he went away happily. Later, Bert returned explaining he had been to Torquay to see the accountant.

When I explained what I had done, he was at first put out thinking I had taken my position too far but he soon let it lie. When he later heard from Robin, who explained how well the new fertiliser was working and what a good decision it had been to go for it on that day, Bert conceded that I had done the right thing.

Later, when he took me to visit two of his farms, he noted how easily I communicated with the farmers and understood the workings of the estates. Finally, we went to visit one of the tenants in their house in Ashburton and while he had nothing much to say to them, he noted how I engaged with them happily.

Bert was a lovely man but he did not have the natural habit of small talk with practically anyone but me. This was something that came naturally to me however. Therefore, shortly after these visits he came to me with a proposal.

"I have let the business falter somewhat since the death of Doris. I was not inclined to get involved in the day-to-day running or to do anything with managing the estates or properties, so I have largely left that to my attorney and the new estate manager.

You have that natural instinct on how to work with people and to see what the solutions should be. Would you like to get involved with the business?"

I couldn't believe what I was hearing but I was delighted.

From that day forward, I dealt with all the elements of the business which necessitated dealing with human beings whereas Bert dealt with all the financial and legal elements. We were the perfect team. It took me a little while to get up to speed with what the actual business was and how to deal with people in the 1920s but soon everything was working well.

Although I was putting my faith in one man to manage all the monetary side of my life once more, things were totally different with Bert compared to what they had been with John. For one, Bert was a proper gentleman who truly loved me more than he did himself and secondly, without me, Bert would not be able to manage his business. I had found my niche, and in 1921 of all times!

That didn't mean of course that all my problems were solved, in fact many were just beginning to start.

There were so many things that I took for granted in 2021 which were not possible or much more difficult in 1921.

Of course, there was no mobile phone, no television, no Internet to check things up on (that did come to frustrate me on occasion) and no modern cars and road infrastructure to make travelling around very easy. However, most of these I came to regard as being blessings rather than curses.

A mobile phone was a very handy thing to have but also such a tie. I quickly found that, although I missed not having the world at my fingertips, being able to get away from text messages and phone calls was a real blessing.

There were a few things that I missed by not having a television and a few times I did crave my "crappy" films but I was amazed how quickly I got into the routine of actually talking to Bert in the evening, something that John and I very rarely did. We would also snuggle up in front of the fire reading books to each other and in later years we would listen to the wireless but I also got into the same timeframe as Bert, which meant that I went to bed earlier and got up earlier and began to enjoy the delights of Devon at dawn. Nature's bounty was often much better than anything television could produce.

At first I did miss my car but i soon came to love travelling by train. Amazingly the trains seem to run on time and although we would sometimes get smothered by the smoke and ash, they were usually a joy to travel on. So much more relaxed than driving and surprisingly quick. Plus we were fortunate that Mr Beeching had not yet been able to wield his axe yet, therefore so many more places were accessible by train, including the direct train from Torquay to Moretonhampstead.

Whilst I was able to cope with some things, others were not so easy.

The first came up almost immediately, as my time of the month started just a couple of days after my decision to stay in 1921. I hadn't thought to bring any sanitary products with me, so I was left with a dilemma – risk heading back to 2021 or try and sort out something here and now.

I decided on the latter. I had in my head an idea from school that ladies had used "rags" before the advent of property sanitary products. But an obvious question was when sanitary products were actually invented. There was no point asking Bert, therefore with some trepidation, I approached Mrs Holmes.

"Erm, Mrs Holmes? I have a rather delicate question to ask you."

She looked at me with her usual disdain. "Yes?"

"Where can i obtain products to help with my period?"

She looked at my blankly this time. I realised that "period" must not be in common usage in 1921.

"Sorry I mean my menstrual cycle."

This time she looked at me with shock, then disgust, shook her head and walked away. I was left standing there all alone and no further forward. What should i do?

I needed to find something, so later that evening I decided to raid the kitchens and store rooms to see what there was. Bert was in the drawing room and i had no idea where Mr and Mrs Holmes lurked when they were not working (though they did have their own day quarters on the very top floor), so i made my way in tentatively.

The kitchens did not prove too successful. There were some cloths in there but they were all used and mainly for protecting your hands when carrying hot pots. Next to the kitchen was the laundry room. I had just started rummaging when I heard a noise in the kitchen. I stopped moving and tried not to breathe. I could hear the faint sound of footsteps and then was able to spy Mrs Holmes carrying a ceramic jug. I ducked down behind a large cabinet, so that I could no longer be seen, however if she entered the room I would be spotted and would have some explaining to do. I continued to hold my breath.

Eventually she left once more and I was able to resume my searching. I did find some cotton flannelette and some scissors and decided that was my best bet for that evening.

The next day I headed to Newton Abbot and was delighted to see that there was a Boots there. I made my way in to the shop and was even more pleased to see lots of products on shelves and tables, which meant that I could wander around and see if anything met my needs. The man behind the counter looked at me warmly and greeted me, I acknowledged him back.

I made my way around the store and found many things but nothing that looked like feminine hygeine products. Dispirited, I looked towards the counter and the rows of products behind the serving man. Could what I wanted be up there?

Could i ask?

I felt like a teenager once more. Eventually i decided to bite the bullet and go up and ask.

"Erm, sorry to ask but do you have any products for feminine hygeine?"

"Sorry Madam, what do you mean by feminine hygeine?" the shop assistant looked slightly wary as he asked this.

"Oh you know, for when a lady has her time of the month." I replied.

It took a moment but then the realisation dawned on his face and he looked at me with the most neutral look i had ever received.

"No Madam, we do not have anything of that kind here in Boots." And he actually turned away from me and started to do something else.

So the rags it was to be. I did try broaching the subject with my doctor a few months later and he seemed even more annoyed with me than Mrs Holmes or the shop assistant.

A few years later some new products were advertised in the ladies magazines that I had started to take but i had found that i had got used to my rags routine and not long after that, the menopause kicked in and soon there was no need for that type of product anyway, though the menopause brought its own unique challenges of course...

It did seem that the 1920s were easier for men!

Other problems were much more mundane but no less annoying at times. Not being able to walk into a hot shower, irritated me for at least two years. At the other end of the spectrum, the lack of fridge and freezer was a frustration too, though you quickly learned to eat what was ripe and ready now. To be honest, Mrs Holmes wouldn't let me linger in the kitchen for long anyway, that was very much her domain. However she did soon come to realise that I had a need for coffee and fruit juice every morning, the latter came freshly squeezed!

CHAPTER FORTY

Outside of work, our lives were fairly idyllic. I could walk down to the beach to swim whenever I wanted to, and we would walk along the coastline or take the carriage or train to Torquay, Newton Abbot, Exeter, Totnes and Plymouth.

We had a small group of good friends. Although they were more Bert's friends than mine and despite me not adhering to the model of what a middle-class lady should be and do, I actually found I liked a lot of them and we had some good times together.

The main thing though was Bert and I. We were inseparable. We had our arguments, of course, and I even spent a week sleeping in one of the spare bedrooms after one particularly vehement argument. However, largely we were perfect together.

One of the issues that kept coming up between us was when I wanted things to be better than they were. I finally persuaded Bert to have proper indoor toilets installed but he went to a local company who didn't have the experience of doing it properly. I spoke to some other friends of ours, who had done it properly and found out that they had used a different company who were based in Newton Abbot. Bert had baulked at the original cost of having them installed and went absolutely crazy when he heard that I wanted to start again but eventually he conceded to me. When they were finally properly up and running, he grudgingly decided to agree with me.

One thing he did concede on straight away was our vegetarianism. He went vegetarian from day one and stayed that way. Even when we had guests to dine, we served only vegetarian food and he brought in a cook who had worked in India to support Mrs Holmes as her capabilities were being sorely tested.

We were living in the so-called 'Roaring Twenties' but living in Devon, we were much removed from the frivolity and excesses that were happening in London, Paris and New York. True, we did occasionally go to dances at the best hotels in Torquay and dance the Charleston. Also, we did go to the cinema to hear Al Jolson sing and talk in The Jazz Singer but largely the life in Devon went on much as before.

The one thing that didn't change for me was swimming. As I've already mentioned we did enjoy going swimming and I was delighted that Bert came to share my passion. At first he thought it a bit odd that I would swim three or four times a week and would come along with me but not always join in.

Then it all changed when we went to visit Sharrah Pool in late July. It was a lovely warm day and he had some work to do with his estate manager in Ashburton. We took the horse carriage from Newton Abbot to Ashburton, the journey was nothing like i remembered from the 21st Century. The outskirts of Newton Abbot finished much earlier than ever before. Highweek was very much a separate village and of course there was no A38 to make the journey pass by more quickly.

Bert's meeting was at 10am and he was done much more quickly than he expected, so we bought some cheese, fruit, bread and cider at the various shops in Ashburton town and arranged for a taxi to take us to New Bridge. The layout at New Bridge was very different to what I remembered but there was still a pathway on the Ashburton side of the bridge, so we decided to take that and see where we ended up.

The pathway had changed, or to get my grammar in the correct order, it hadn't changed yet. Sometimes it is difficult to talk about things happening in the future before the past!

As long as we kept the river on our right and walked for about three quarters of an hour, I knew we would be in about the right place. After a bit of scrambling and rock hopping at the wrong spot, we rounded a bend and found Sharrah Pool ahead of us.

As I hoped there was not a soul there. I changed into my modern swimming costume but Bert just stripped down to his drawers and even kept his hat on at first. I laughed and told him to take off his hat and we both got into the water.

To me, it felt deliciously warm after the warming effects of the sunshine and warm air on the dark water but to Bert it was obviously cold and he gave a little yelp. His arms came out in goose pimples and he held his arms tightly around his chest. I looked at him with a mixture of love and delight at his discomfort, remembering my similar experiences a year or so before.

I swam out into the deep water and after a short while he followed me and surprised me with his adept swimming ability. He later explained to me that he had swum many times as a child and had become quite proficient but never really kept it up when he became an adult.

We both swam up towards the little waterfall and I showed him how to enjoy the fast flow of the water and get a back massage. We then climbed up on to the rocks and jumped in. We swam up and down the pool and basically had a delightful time.

After a while I decided to get out but Bert seemed reluctant. "Come on Bert or else you will catch a chill" I called out to him.

Out of the water there was little or no chance of catching a chill as the air temperature was so warm. Because no one came to disturb our peace, we were able to strip out of our wet things and dry ourselves in the warm sunshine. Even though we thought no one would come, we still took off our wet items and put on our underwear before eating our lovely lunch. I felt more in tune with nature than I had even been before. Sharing it with Bert made it even more magical.

After lunch, we lay in the sunshine once more and this time I surprised Bert by tracing my fingers across his bare chest. I must assume that Doris had never initiated any sexual activity, as he watched me and didn't say a word. It was the most delightful sensual and sexual experience of my life. Nothing with John or even Bert had ever come close. I felt like a teenager experiencing excitement for the first time and we even carried on in the river when we got in once more to cool off.

That afternoon not only re-initiated Bert's love for swimming, it made us even closer as lovers than either of us had been with partners before.

Neither of us wanted to leave but time was marching on, so eventually we headed back to New Bridge. That would normally have been the cue for me to get in the car and drive home but obviously we didn't have that luxury in 1921. Nor did we have mobiles phones to call for a taxi. Therefore it was Shank's pony for us and we headed back towards Ashburton.

Fortunately after only about a mile of walking, a carter came along who offered us a lift on the back of his cart. For some reason this delighted Bert and I even more, so we laughed and drank the rest of the cider with another piece of cheese each. I smiled as we navigated the narrow section of road (towards what would become the River Dart Country Park), because we passed through totally unhindered. Whereas in 2021 you would need to stop every few yards to pass another car coming the other way.

The carter dropped us off in Ashburton and unasked for, Bert gave him a sixpence, which brought about a doffing of the hat from the delighted man. We had timed it pretty much perfectly to get the carriage back to Newton Abbot, where we caught the train to Torquay and finally got a cab back home to end an absolutely delightful day.

After that day, Bert came swimming with me pretty much every time!

CHAPTER FORTY ONE

My knowledge of the inter war period was fairly limited. I knew that there was a Wall Street crash in the late 1920s but was not quite sure when it would happen exactly. When I heard that stock prices were skyrocketing, I dropped some hints to Bert that prices could not go on rising forever and eventually in the summer of 1929 he cashed in most of his shares.

His stock broker said that he was crazy, that the market was extremely buoyant and that Bert should start to re-invest immediately. He continued to pester Bert who was beginning to waver during September. However, just in time, for us at least, the London Stock Exchange crashed with stock prices plummeting.

I was surprised to hear that the Wall Street market hadn't crashed and stocks started to rise once more but then at the end of October the actual Wall Street Crash happened.

Although we had escaped ruin, which had happened to many of our contemporaries, the years that followed were still years of austerity after the extravagances of the 'Roaring Twenties'. Some of Bert's tenants could no longer afford their rents and we had to let them miss some of their payments or have no tenants at all. This was the same for our tenant farmers as it was for the housing tenants.

This situation was mirrored all over the country. Poverty was rife and as the 1920s turned into the 1930s, the country seemed to be in a constant state of worry and strife. It was not an uncommon thing to see homeless people living by the roadside in makeshift shacks. I even saw a dead body lying in the road once or twice. One had obviously been there for days before the authorities came to clear the body away to be buried in a pauper's grave.

The sadness of the country was not mirrored in our household. If anything, Bert and I were almost more in love with each other than before. We were both now in our fifties and had fitted together like two pieces from a jigsaw. He continued joining me in my winter morning swims as well as those from May to November when the water was at its warmest.

In 1932 I heard a word and a name that I did know all about though. Bert was reading the morning paper and often he would read out articles that he thought would be of interest to me. He summarised for me, "in Germany they have had another election, but the new runner, Adolf Hitler, has failed in his bid to oust von Hinderburg."

A shiver ran down my spine at his name.

Bert, unaware of my reaction, continued, "I'm not sure what they believe in over there but apparently they seem to want to fight to achieve it. At least if the Germans are all fighting amongst themselves they won't want to fight with us again."

I shook my head, knowing what was to follow.

A few months later he was reading the paper again. "Remember that German Hitler chap, it turns out his party has won the latest election. They now rule Germany and are making big changes over there. The paper thinks there is going to be a civil war over there. The best thing though is that they are anti-Bolshevist and will stop the spread of communism through Europe. There will be war in Europe again, mark my words, but we won't be involved. It will be the fascists fighting the Bolsheviks."

I decided to keep quiet. In some ways of course he was right and Hitler didn't really want to fight with the British (who he considered to be potential allies against the Slavs and Communists) but his imperialist ambitions would bring him up against us.

CHAPTER FORTY TWO

Bert and I continued to spend most of our time together, which was a new found joy for me and also for him too. We would swim most days at Lemoncombe. It took him a while to show the same passion for it as I did. At first i think he was just doing it to keep me happy, for such was his nature, but soon he seemed to show as much passion for it as I did.

As well as visiting Lemoncombe we would sometimes go further afield. In the 1920s and 1930s it was not so easy to get to some of the locations I would regularly have visited in the 2020s. Travelling times were so much longer without fast cars and fast roads, though other places were more reachable by train. The first time we went to Moretonhampstead I was delighted to make the journey by train.

Other locations were reachable but were not accessible. Of course there were public footpaths back then but the National Trust was still quite young, so many of the locations opened up by them, such as the Teign below Castle Drogo or some of the beaches in South Devon, could only be accessed via private land and therefore with the permission of the landowner. Of course, many people just ignored this and headed to these places anyway but sometimes there would be nasty gamekeeper or farmer willing to fire their shotgun.

Bert came into his own here though, he did seem to know more people than i realised at first. When he and his first wife had been younger, they had been more closely involved in the socialite world of Edwardian Torquay and Newton Abbot. In this time, Bert had made many acquaintances and some were quite influential.

One of these was to delight me most specially in 1933. We had now been married for over 12 years but our love was still strong and young. Bert continued to delight me with little things and every now and then he would pull an even bigger rabbit out of the bag.

He announced on Tuesday 11th July 1933 that we would be taking a little trip at the weekend but would not be pressed on the destination. He advised me on what to bring and wear but otherwise the location was a mystery. I knew we would be going away for five nights from the Thursday to the Tuesday and that the journey would include a boat journey from Torquay to Dartmouth and then on to Salcombe but that was all.

True enough, we arranged a cab (now motorised) to collect us from home and take us to Torquay Harbour, where we joined a ferry service which took us to Dartmouth, here we stopped for lunch and then the ferry carried on to Salcombe.Finally another cab (this time horse driven) picked us up and took us inland through the lanes of the South Hams. We travelled alone, so the cab driver had to lift our quite extensive luggage off the boat and on to his cab.

The journey through the lanes of the South Hams was quite delightful. The July sun was warm but not too hot. The birds were singing and the summer flowers were in bloom. I tried to work out where we were but without the same road signs, and with very different looking roads, some of the familiar locations looked very different. We didn't seem to pass through any major villages or small towns, which may have enlightened me.

It was only as we neared the coastline again that I had an inkling of where we were. This time there were some signs indicating directions to Bigbury and Challaborough. We passed through the hamlet of Bigbury and then we were at Bigbury on Sea looking across to Burgh Island.

"That is where we are staying for next few nights." Bert announced, pointing towards the hotel on Burgh Island. If we hadn't been in public I would have grabbed him to me and kissed him. Oh what the hell? I did it anyway!

CHAPTER FORTY THREE

July 1933 – Burgh Island

I was expecting to see the tractor take us over from Bigbury to Burgh Island but instead a rather swish looking wooden motor boat took us and two other hotel guests.

They were younger than us and turned out to be an attorney and his wife down from London. They had friends already staying at the hotel and planned to join them for a few days. Bert explained that we were staying for four nights and were here to relax and swim. I echoed this, saying that I had wanted for many years to visit the island but never had.

It didn't take long to reach the Island and soon we were disembarking from the small motor boat and making our way up the jetty.

A porter took our baggage up to the hotel on a hand cart and the four of us made our way up the steps, directed by another porter who hurried on ahead of us. When we reached the veranda, a gentleman came out to greet us "Mr and Mrs Windyett?" he looked towards us and we nodded. "Mr and Mrs Thomas?" this time it was the other couple who nodded.

He then indicated towards a set off comfortable chairs and a table "Would you care for a refreshment after your climb? Pimms, Gin & It or perhaps Lemonade?"

I was a little to eager to answer "Pimms please." Bert looked at me and smiled "The same for me, if you would be so kind." The Thomas's also placed their orders and the four of us sat in the comfortable chairs overlooking the sea.

It was mid-afternoon and the Sun was shining brightly. There were very few craft out on the sea and the sun rippled on the small waves which followed them. We could just about make out some people below us cavorting in the sea, while behind us we could hear the sounds of people playing tennis to the side of the hotel.

The hotel itself was majestic. An art deco masterpiece in white atop a rocky outcrop off the South Devon coast. Everywhere you looked was an amazing vista over looking the sea or the South Devon coastline. A man in a white tuxedo brought our drinks, Bert and I chinked our glasses and I felt like I was in heaven on earth.

We were not rushed at all but after a while, the same man who had greeted us originally approached us from the hotel. "Would you care to see your rooms?"

All four of us nodded and he turned on his heels and led us back up to the hotel. We barely paused in the foyer before making our way up the stairway. Miraculously another man appeared at the top of the stairs and said "Mr and Mrs Thomas, this way if you would be so kind." He then led them off in another direction, while we followed the original man along a corridor.

He stopped at a door, which opened on to a suite which took my breath away. The facilities would be seen as basic to modern eyes (there was a bathroom, which was literally just a bath, sink and toilet) but the decor was glorious. The bed, dressing tables and chairs were cut into geometric shapes of cedarwood. The colour scheme was deep blue and gold and was accentuated by the cushions, lamp shades and wall paper behind the bed.

The large bed faced an even larger window which opened out on to a private balcony and this in turn housed a set of table and two chairs. I had to walk out and savour the even better view we had from our window, which looked back over Bigbury towards Bantham beach and beyond to Bolt Tail.

I noticed Bert handing the hotel man some money and waited for him to leave before wandering across to Bert. Putting my arms around him, I said "Thank you my darling Bert, you have made a dream finally come true."

He just smiled and said "the chap said that dinner would be served at 7:30pm, shall we have a little walk and then come back to freshen up before we head down?"

I agreed, so we decided to head straight down as we were both wearing confortable shoes and clothing. We made our way to the foyer and were just making for the doors out of the hotel when a female voice behind us said "Bertie, Bertie Windyett, is that you?"

We both turned and a a brown haired lady and a man with a pencil moustache were walking towards us. They were both slightly younger than us and I looked towards Bert who showed no initial sign of recognition.

The lady spoke once more in a clear and crisp voice "It is you Bertie. Do you not remember me? It's Agatha, you were good friends with my sister Madge Miller back in Torquay some twenty years ago."

"Agatha Miller!" exclaimed Bertie. "Well I never. I haven't seen you in years."

"Well." The lady replied. " I have been living away for some time but we..." she linked arms with the man at this point "...are hoping to return to live in Devon again soon. This is my husband Max Mallowan. Max, this is Bertie Windyett, whom we used to know in Torquay before the war."

Names started to pop into my head. Agatha, Mallowan, Torquay, Burgh Island. My instincts were confirmed when Bert replied. "Agatha, Mr Mallowan may I introduce my wife Olivia. Olivia, I'd like you to meet an old friend, Agatha Christie."

The name hung in the air for a moment light as a feather but hit me with the full force of a wrecking ball.

Agatha Christie!
Agatha Christie?
AGATHA CHRISTIE!

"I tend to go under the name of Mrs Mallowan hereabouts." said the lady in question but then her husband interjected.

"But everyone knows my wife as Agatha Christie, so there is no need to feel any contrition."

Agatha smiled at Max and we all shared a gentle laugh before Mr Mallowan continued "Have you just arrived today?" We nodded. "In that case, you must join us tonight for dinner, we have a small party and it would be delightful to have two more."

I looked at Bert eagerly, he nodded and then replied "I can speak for both of us, we would be delighted to join you."

Dinner with Agatha Christie?

Could this trip get any better?

CHAPTER FORTY FOUR

We did go for our walk but i barely took in the beautiful surroundings. Bert tried to engage me in small talk but all I could think about was Agatha Christie. Agatha Christie!

He explained that when he and Doris had been newly married they were part of the Torquay scene of middle class families. One of these families was the Millers, who eldest child Margaret was a similar age to Doris and therefore they became friends. Margaret, or "Madge" as she was known, had a younger sister called Agatha who would later become Agatha Christie.

I tried to recollect my knowledge about the history of Agatha Christie but was not sure where 1933 fitted into that history. I knew that she was already famous, because she was already well-known when she split up with her first husband (obviously called Mr Christie) and then she went missing for a number of days. She was now with her second husband Max, with whom she would live at Greenway House in Devon and travel to Mesopotamia doing archaeological research.

That was about it. A few year's earlier I had bought a first edition of "The Murder at the Vicarage" which was the first Miss Marple story and I also had a couple of the Poirot stories but I could not be sure which stories were still to be written. For example had she written "And then there were none" or "Evil under the sun" yet? Both of these I knew were said to be based here at Burgh

Island. What about "Murder on the Orient Express" or "Death on the Nile"? Were they early books or later ones?

I was not sure and decided to try not to mention them.

We headed back to the hotel and got ourselves ready for dinner. I was so eager, I was actually ready by 7pm. Bert was good enough not to mention this fact, as traditionally he would be sitting waiting for me to get ready.

Dinner in the 1930s was a very different thing and dinner on Burgh Island in the 1930s was even more different. First we were directed into a room where there were a number of waiters walking around with a variety of cocktails and canapés.

Max came over and introduced us to Mr and Mrs Taylor, who would also be joining us at dinner. We all confirmed that we had already met on the boat trip over to the island and Max explained that Mr Thomas was his attorney and was here as his guest.

He looked around the room. "It doesn't appear that our other guests have made an appearance yet."

Of course I wanted to chat to Agatha but at first i decided to play it cool and what was I to say anyway?

In the end the decision was made for me, as Bert and Agatha got together to chat about "the old times" in Torquay, while Max and Mr Thomas chatted together, therefore it was left to myself and Florence Thomas to talk.

She had never left London before, so we ended up talking about the travails of travelling, the delights of Devon and the prospects of what was to come at dinner. The latter was soon to become apparent as we were called through to the next room for dinner itself.

In all there were about thirty people dining there that evening and we were directed to a table laid out for eight of those people but as we sat down there were still only six of us. Bert was sitting between Agatha and myself but on my other side there were two spaces.

Aperitifs were served and then came the starters. The party were very interested in my being vegetarian and Bert's conversion. Agatha seemed very interested in this. "I have often thought." she said "That a vegetarian would make a truly unique detective. I have found many vegetarians to be savants and therefore they would be erudite enough to find solutions where others could not. It would not be right for Poirot but perhaps i will make another of my characters vegetarian at some point."

I remembered these words when I later read about Ariadne Oliver's detective Sven in a later Poirot book, who was a vegetarian.

Just as we were digesting these words a voice drifted across to our table from a few feet away.

"You must forgive us dear people. Gertie was telling me all about New York and I did not have the heart to interrupt her and explain we were going to be late for dinner."

That voice was so distinct. It was unique. I knew who exactly was joining us.

Walking towards us, arm in arm were a man wearing a perfect suit, bow tie, slicked back hair and smile and a lady with tight curls in her hair, a long flowing floral dress and lit cigarette protruding almost one foot from her mouth in a black cigarette holder.

The lady would have been unknown to me before my travelling back in time but in the 1920s and 30s, everyone knew Gertrude Lawrence. The man and his voice were known to me whether I was living in the 1920s or 2020s. He pulled out the chair next to Mr Thomas for Gertrude to sit in and then moved to the chair next to me, taking my hand as he took his seat he kissed it gently and then said "Delighted to meet you my dear, my name is Noel Coward!".

The next couple of hours were a complete blur. I was sharing dinner with Agatha Christie, Noel Coward and Gertrude Lawrence. No disrespect to Max and the Thomas's intended.

Noel Coward was a delight. He seemed to find something interesting to say about everything i told him. He had obviously overheard about my being vegetarian. "I am afraid my dear, that the life of the vegetarian is not for me but i doff my hat to any who can take the plunge."

He also was very interested in my thoughts about Herr Hitler and I found myself using my knowledge of history to say more than I should just to impress this man who was so impressive himself.

After explaining that I thought that Herr Hitler would not only have designs on the lands that Germany had lost at the Treaty of Versailles but would also like to unite Austria and Germany into one powerful nation, Mr Coward spoke out loud to the whole table "I often hear it mooted that the fair sex are less intelligent than their male counterparts. The evidence of this table illustrates that this is a pure fallacy created by misogynistic and ignorant men who are worried that they will be usurped and left struggling to understand their place in society." He nodded to Agatha, Gertrude and myself in turn before alighting on Mrs Thomas "Please forgive me Florence, Agatha and Gertrude have had their intelligence shine brightly for many years, while Olivia here is showing more knowledge on international affairs than many of our so-called best diplomats, whereas you and I have not had the opportunity for intercourse as yet. When we do I am sure you will enlighten me with the proof for Fermat's theorem or tell me the age of the universe but until that point i will merely bask in the glories of these three fine women."

For a moment no-one spoke and then Gertrude let out a huge laugh, which made other tables turn to look and which set us all off laughing.

I have never spent an evening like it. Agatha and Gertrude were indeed erudite, intelligent and very interesting but i realised that Noel Coward was almost directing the conversations around the table. Whenever someone would struggle with something to say or talk about, he would interject with a witty remark or a leading question which would get things started again.

For pure wit, Gertrude was his match but for quickness of brain, he was sometimes outsmarted by Agatha but this did not seem to bother him. In fact he delighted in it, having others who could keep up with him and even outshine him from time to time was perhaps a relief.

I found that I barely chatted to Bert, for when I was not talking to Noel or to Florence (who sat opposite me), I found I was delighting in listening to the repartee of others.

The meal that was served to us was fabulous but, on this occasion, it paled into insignificance compared to the company.

The next few days were also a delight. We spent more time chatting, walking and dining with Agatha, Noel, Gertrude and others on the island but Bert and I also managed to have some quality time alone.

On the third day, Bert came to me after breakfast with a a full knapsack on his back. "Today we are walking to some of the coves" he declared.

What followed was the best day of the trip and even outshone meeting Agatha and Noel. We walked to some hidden coves, swam alone in the azure sea and then had a picnic with just the two of us on the beach. Bert had even managed to secure a bottle of Champagne and two flutes. Even though the Champagne was no longer cold, we drank it on the beach while nibbling the ripe strawberries and i realised why i was so deeply in love with this man.

All too soon, our short break on Burgh Island was over. We made our farewells to the Mallowans and the Thomases and others (Noel and Gertrude had already left the day before). Before heading down to the quayside.

Bert and I enjoyed many other short breaks but none was quite like that one.

CHAPTER FORTY FIVE

The next few years were very difficult in some ways, but easy in others. The Great Depression had different effects on different parts of the country. The industrial hubs of London, the Midlands, and the North struggled terribly and the newspapers and radio continued to report on the awful hardships and poverty.

Whereas down here in the South West, after an initial period of hardship, rural agriculture started to prosper and we were better off towards the end of the 1930s than we were at the start of the decade.

My thoughts, however, were heavy with the impending doom of 1939.

Although Hitler and Nazis were newsworthy and there was some worry when they started re-building their Navy and Air Force, there seemed to be more coverage of the Spanish Civil War, than the rise of Nazi Germany. Following the events in Spain, some British people were worried about the rise of the communists and others were worried by the rise of right wingers.

Bert knew some men who had decided to go and fight on the side of the Republicans but two of them returned after a few months, moaning about the 'Bloody Russkis' (Russian communists were supporting the Spanish communists with money, armaments and "morale") . There was also a young man who lived down the road who went to fight on the side of the Nationalists (led by

Franco) but he never returned.

Italy invaded Abyssinian and then Germany merged with Austria in the “Anschluss”. They followed this by threatening to invade the Sudetenland in Czechoslovakia. Although Neville Chamberlain came back with promises of “peace in our time” from the Munich peace talks, everyone started gearing up for a potential war with Germany.

Some people seemed quite positive about “bashing the Bosch” once more but those who had fought in the previous war started to have nightmares once more. One of these was Bert. He told me all about it one evening.

“You can not imagine the horrors of war, Livvy. Death was commonplace, as was hunger, disease and inhumanity. I saw things that I would not wish on my worst enemy and I have done things that I am not proud of.

If we go to war with Germany, it will all happen again. Young men will die and even those that do return home will never actually leave the battlefields.”

He said more but I would not recount it to everybody. It was the private musings of just one of many who were scarred for life by the horrors that they saw and experienced. All I could do was to hug this special man and pray that things would not be so bad this time around.

On the 1st September 1939 Germany invaded Poland. Britain gave Germany an ultimatum to withdraw and when they didn't we all gathered around the radio in the morning of the 3rd September to hear Neville Chamberlain make an announcement.

Although I heard the words many times in my life before, to actually hear them at the time they were read out and knowing what was to come, hit me like a hammer blow. What also surprised me was that Chamberlain's words did not end with the line "...and that consequently, this country is at war with Germany."

He actually went on to explain that he had tried his best to prevent war and how sorry he was that the country would be put through it all again. I suddenly had a new deep felt respect for this man who had been so disrespected by history. He, like Bert, could remember the horrors of the previous war and tried everything he could to prevent it happening again. Whereas Churchill seemed to take an unnatural delight in the fear and tension that war created.

What surprised me most, however, was how slowly the war actually happened. There were changes of course. Later that month there was a national register of everyone in the country, so the Government would know who could do what in support of the war effort. Plus we were all issued with 'identity cards'. Then we were given gas masks and attended local meetings on how to use them and what to do in the event of an air raid.

Petrol was rationed and so our car stayed in the garage. When we first got the car it annoyed Bert slightly that I learned how to drive it more quickly than he did and so it became 'my car'. Not that it mattered now, as it was just gathering dust.

Even though all this was happening in preparation, little actual war was happening in our lives. I did join other local ladies at Newton Abbot train station to provide food and clothing to Polish and Czech people who arrived destitute at Plymouth, after escaping the Nazis.

But otherwise there was not much going on war-wise on a day to day basis and our lives were barely changed for months.

In April, Germany invaded Norway and Denmark, and for the first time Allied forces engaged the Germans but with little success. The start of the war happened in earnest though when the Germans marched into the Low Countries and totally bypassed France's Maginot Line.

Within days Chamberlain had resigned, Churchill had taken over a National Government and Bert and many others had joined the "Local Defence Volunteers" after a radio announcement by Anthony Eden. They would later be called the 'Home Guard' and of course be known in Britain as the "Dad's Army". Bert was made a Sergeant based on his WWI experience and I tried not to compare him with John Le Mesurier, even though his Captain was a short man with glasses!

France fell in just a few weeks, the British army achieved a heroic withdrawal from Dunkirk, which the newspapers lauded as if it was a victory. Then the war hit us all. Everything was rationed even more tightly than before and everyone started seeing spies and traitors behind every hedge. There was also a genuine fear that the Germans would invade us and none of my gainsaying would stop people thinking that it would happen any day soon.

I joined the Women's Volunteer Service and when they found out that I had a car and could drive, I was given extra petrol rations and was tasked with a number of roles as my car became a staff car to the local service officers. In effect I became their chauffeur, we even had a special telephone installed in our home so that I could be contacted at short notice to go and collect some officer or other and take him to another location.

Bert took this new role in my life with equanimity and would boast of his wife "who is doing more in the war than I am" though he was careful not to say exactly what. "Careless talk costs lives" and all that.

It was in these dark days of war, that I started to forget about the life I had lived before this. At no point did I think "Why don't I escape this war and return back to 2021?" This was my life now and all I cared about was helping the war effort and looking after

Bert.

I was not even sure if I could return to 2021 but even if I could, life here during World War II with Bert was preferable to a safer life alone in 2021.

CHAPTER FORTY SIX

That is not to say that the next five years were not hard for me, for Bert, or for others. I was terrified when we encountered our first air raid, which happened when I drove a Brigadier to catch a train in Newton Abbot. To see the bombs actually landing, buildings being destroyed, and the aftermath of dead and injured people was very sobering.

We would often see the bombers flying over our house and we could see the vapour trails from dogfights out to sea some times.

The main hardship for us though was the rationing, though we were luckier than most because of our chickens. We decided to convert much of our garden to growing vegetables, which helped even more. This was something I had done before in my house I had shared with John, so I had a headstart over many others of our middle class contemporaries. We also benefited from a few special things which sometimes found their way from Bert's farms to our table. Though of course we stayed vegetarian, we lived on eggs for our protein at this time.

The war dragged on and on. People began to think that it would never end, even when the Americans finally joined in. There were heroes to get excited about, like Monty in North Africa, but there were also failures such as Arthur Percival in Singapore, a defeat that rocked Britain to the core. Would we lose our Empire and have to change the colours on the maps from pink?

I tried to keep everyone upbeat, declaring that Hitler had overstretched himself by attacking the Soviet Union, just like

Napoleon a century or so earlier but when their troops marched straight through the Russian defences, many declared that Hitler would soon rule from the Atlantic to the Pacific.

Bit by bit, the tide started to turn though. There was not one defining moment but we began to hear of successes in the Mediterranean, in North Africa, in Greece and the Partisans efforts in Yugoslavia. The Allies managed a few successes against a previously undefeatable Japanese and public opinion began to be more positive. Of course no one knew about how important things like Radar or Bletchley Park were, because they were not reported to the general public (or practically anyone) at that time.

A few times I would say things like “only two years more of this war” or “we will invade France next year” to which Bert would look at me strangely but not say anything.

In June 1944 D-Day happened and we all celebrated but again things did not happen as quickly as I imagined. Of course I knew that the war did not end until 1945 but I imagined it was inevitable that we would win after D-Day. Then came the German counter offensives which dragged on for months, ending with the carnage of the Battle of the Bulge.

In 1945 things seemed to improve almost day by day but then some of the news of the horrors of what the Nazis had been up to started to permeate through the media as the concentration camps were liberated. Up until that point we still knew people who would talk about “the bloody Jews, they deserve it” but when even those people heard what was going on and saw the newsreels, they hung their heads in shame.

On May 8th we all celebrated the end of the war in Europe but there were still horrors to come. The Yanks, Aussies and Brits were pushing back the Japanese but still they would not surrender. Then on the 6th August the Americans dropped an atomic bomb on Hiroshima and devastated the city. Still the Japanese did not capitulate and three days later another bomb was dropped on Nagasaki. When everyone heard how many people had been killed and that most of them were ordinary Japanese citizens, they went white with horror.

The actual war was over but the aftermath would last for years to come.

CHAPTER FORTY SEVEN

Again I knew a little bit about the post war period but not too much. I had to laugh about how angry Bert got when Atlee and the Labour Party won the 1945 election defeating Churchill and the Tories.

"Bloody ingrates." Bert said. "Churchill saved this country and they go and vote for a bloody communist!"

Bert didn't swear very often, so I always found it amusing when he did. But this and other things did seem to weigh more heavily on him than they would have done in the past. In early 1945 he turned 70, but to me (who was used to how people aged in the 21st Century) he was looking more like a man of 80.

I myself was now 69, though I still found it hard to work out how old I was. When I lived in 2021 I would work out how old I was by working forward from 1975, which was my year of birth. I had to keep on remembering that my new "birth year" was 1875. It should have been easy really but for some reason the hundred years difference confused me.

Anyway, Bert was looking and acting older and the post war austerity continued and some things were even harder. The Government was broke, all the servicemen returned and the women didn't want to give up their jobs.

After a few years, even though we still had rationing and

austerity, things did seem to improve with positive news though. The welfare state was announced in 1948 and suddenly everyone was looked after much more effectively than before. I benefited almost straight away when I was called in for an opticians appointment and given “National Health Glasses”. Bert didn't think I should have them but I was sort of proud to be there at the start of that amazing institution and delighted to wear them.

Bert also visited the local hospital as an NHS patient when he had a fall outside the house but fortunately it was just a dizzy spell caused when he had got up too quickly.

Bit by bit the things that were being rationed were being reduced and soon it became a delight to go into Newton Abbot and visit the wide variety of shops to browse the products on offer. Some more of the household names that I would know in later days started to appear amongst the High Street shops.

We had a new car and Bert had to concede that it should be left to me to do the driving, as he had barely driven since the 1930s.

In 1952 the King died and the new Elizabethan age started with our new Queen. I was not much of a monarchist but even I got carried away by the feelings of the people about the young Princess and a bright new era. Later that year my own Prince took a turn for the worse and afterwards he hardly ever left the house as he found it hard to stay steady.

The last time I remember him leaving the house was in the Spring of 1953. He had some energy again and decided to walk down to the beach. We watched the waves and the cormorants diving in the water.

“Do you remember that first day when we first met?” He said suddenly.

“Of course I do, my darling. How could I ever forget?”

"You emerged from the water like a Greek goddess and I fell in love with you straight away. All I wanted from that day onwards was to spend the rest of my life with you. I was so worried I would never see you again when you didn't return for days."

"You should have said something to me before."

"I wanted to but couldn't find the right words, until I saw you swim ashore once more. You have made me so very happy, Livvy, thank you."

He was such a lovely man.

CHAPTER FORTY EIGHT

Autumn can be a lovely time of year but also depressing. The colours in the trees can be delightful and sometimes you get an Indian summer with warm weather and warm seas.

That year however, Autumn was just depressing. The skies were dark grey and the weather wet and cold. Everything had a sombre air, and our house was not exempt from that.

Bert was not well and he seemed to know that his remaining time on Earth was minimal. He would call me into his bedroom, we now slept in separate bedrooms as well as separate beds, and ask me to sit with him while he lay in bed listening to the books I would read to him.

"Tell me about the future," he suddenly asked during a reading of the Time Machine by HG Wells.

"What do you mean, my love?" I asked, wondering whether he was wondering what future he had and what would happen to me, if and when he did die.

"I mean, what is the future like? You've lived there, I would like to understand what is going to happen to us all in years to come."

I looked at him like he was some kind of madman. The future. It was almost like a foreign country to me now. Somewhere (or when) I knew about but didn't think about much or have any plans of returning to soon.

I did know about the future but what could Bert mean?

Surely he didn't know anything about my past or my future or whatever the tense should be...

"I'm sorry Bert, I don't quite understand you. What do you mean, when you say I have lived there?"

"Oh Livvy. Don't take me as a fool. I have known for many years that you came to us out of time. Even when I first met you, you were wearing costumes and carrying things that still haven't been invented yet."

I looked at him in shock.

"Then there were the things you didn't know about our time but knew about things that were to come before they had happened."

I shook my head as if to make sure that I was actually hearing all this for real. "I, I, don't know what to say."

"Just tell me the truth." He looked at me with such love that I could not deny him this simple request.

So I told him everything. About swimming through the archway. About swimming in the future. About John Martin. About Covid. About how my love for him made me stay.

And he asked so many questions. Of course he wanted to know about the future but he also wanted to know about the fine details of when I had come here. Where I lived. Who I lived with. I made sure he knew that there was no one else, I had been living in a shared house with a female friend of mine. I didn't think he was ready to learn about Suze being bi-sexual but pretty much everything else I told him.

He took it all in and although the effort was hard on him, it seemed to give him some solace and even contentment. When I left him later that day, he was tired but there was that smile on his face that made me love him even more.

The next day, he sent me to Exeter on an errand to pick up some documents from one of his landlords. I was therefore away from the house most of the day and unaware that his solicitor John Tuck had been to visit.

A few days later Bert died in my arms. I cried and cried until it was too painful to cry any more. I didn't want to let him go. When I went to my bedroom it seemed even more empty than normal, even though Bert had not slept with me in the same bed for a couple of years.

I just lay there all night in some kind of mind fog. I had no idea of what would happen next and what I should do. Part of me felt my life was over but Bert had been very insistent that I shouldn't stop living, just because he was gone. Any thought of carrying on without him was far from my mind at that moment though. I could not even start to think clearly.

CHAPTER FORTY NINE

Bert had organised practically everything to be handled in the event of his death, which was fortunate because I was still struggling to get to grip with the most basic things, since he had died. He had organised his probate and funeral, so that all i had to do was turn up on the day.

It was my first family funeral since my parents had died. Mum was last to go in 2016, Dad just a couple of years earlier in 2013. Since then I'd been very lucky. Bert had no close family and of course my own family in 1921 would not understand their great granddaughter turning up at family funerals decades before she was born.

This was a biggie though. My soul mate of the last 32 years was not coming back. Just the thought of that made me want to join him in the soil but I was not brave enough to take that step.

There were not many at the funeral, just some friends and acquaintances of Bert and myself. Many of our closest friends had already passed on. There were even fewer who came back to the house afterwards. Mrs Holmes had passed on a few years earlier and I hadn't thought to prepare anything. Therefore I just offered around sherry and shorts, so unsurprisingly the guests didn't stay too long.

The only one who did stay was John Tuck, Bert's solicitor. He was my solicitor as well now but I had never really had any dealings with him directly, that had always been Bert's role and somehow I had been happy to go along with this.

I assumed that he had something legal to run through with me and this was, in fact, the case. Talking of cases, he opened his and took out a large paper document.

"This is the last will and testament of Bertrand Windyett, which I have been instructed to read to you after the funeral. Mr Windyett drew up this will with me in the last week of his life and he planned the date of his funeral. He wanted me to make sure you were aware of his final wishes."

How kind of Bert to think about me when he was that ill and how typically compassionate of him. He was the best man I had ever known. I nodded and pointed towards the dining room table and chairs. Tuck sat on one side and myself on the other.

"As you know, Mr Windyett had a large estate, but most of it will be needed to pay the death taxes. In fact once everything has been taken into account, there will be little or nothing to pass on.

I have been instructed by Mr Windyett to let you arrange the funeral and then to ask you to leave the house and all the belongings you have there with immediate effect. Everything you own was bought and paid for by Mr Windyett and must therefore revert to the estate to ensure the satisfactory resolution of any overdue debts and taxes.

I am afraid there is nothing for you. Mr Windyett has said that you can take one set of clothing and your swimming costume but nothing else."

He said all of this in a deadpan voice and with an ashen look on his face.

"I cannot say anything else on the matter. I wish that it was otherwise but the instructions are clear and are written down here if you would care to read them."

His hands were shaking as he passed the will across the table.

I sat in shock. I really did not have any idea of what to do. I stretched out to grab the will and, turning it around, attempted to read the passage he was alluding to but the tears were already welling up in my eyes.

My whole body went limp and my head struck the table. I heard Mr Tuck cry out in distress and rush around the table to come by my side.

"Olivia, I truly wish that it was otherwise but I cannot gainsay what a man decides in his will. I counselled him against it but he was determined and forthright."

I lifted my head and he proffered me his handkerchief but I waved it away.

I had started the day thinking my life was over and now it truly was, but not in any way I could imagine. The man I had loved and trusted for over thirty years had chosen to destroy me in the end and struck a dagger of hate deep into my heart.

I needed fresh air. I took my leave from Mr Tuck and went upstairs and changed into something more suitable and also picked up my swimming costume and towel.

He greeted me in the hallway saying, "I am sorry Olivia but I must be sure that you are taking out nothing more than one set of clothing and your swimming things."

I shook out my towel and swimming costume to show that there was nothing inside. I then stretched out my arms and shouted, "would you like to check me for any hidden loot as well?"

"That will not be necessary Olivia, I trust you. I just had to ask, as I was instructed to do." To give him credit, he looked almost as miserable as I felt at that moment.

I strode out the door. I had no real idea of my intentions. All I knew was for the second time in my life I had been screwed over by a man I trusted.

John, I could believe could act in that way but Bert? He had never shown any inclination towards malice. Could Tuck be mistaken or misguided? Perhaps he had made it all up to grab the estate himself. No, I knew enough of the man to know that wasn't true. What then? Was there something in me that made men act this way towards me?

I found that I was walking down towards the beach. It was where I and Bert had found solace when we needed it. But this time I wanted to get away from the thought of him too.

Without thinking I changed into my swimming costume and plunged into the water. It was cool but not cold. Perhaps I should end it now? I no longer had anything to live for. I wasn't brave enough before the funeral, but what was the point of continuing now? I was destitute and alone in a time which wasn't really my own.

How did someone drown themselves? I started to think. Did they just go under the water and open their mouths, surely they would just float back up to the top again. Perhaps I should swim back in and throw myself off a cliff.

I looked around me and for the first time I noticed that it was a fairly low tide and the archway was present once more. It had been over thirty years since I had come through that way, not knowing how my life would change. It had seemed to change for the better until the very last moments.

An idea popped into my head. Perhaps I should swim back through. I was not sure it would work and what year it would be, perhaps about 2053? What would I find there? Well, it couldn't be much worse than now. What did I have to lose?

I found it harder than before. Although I was fitter than most people my age, I was now a lady in her seventies and found swimming out that far a bit more of a challenge than I would have liked. There was also a bit of a current working against me, so that when I finally reached the archway I was a bit out of breath. I paused before swimming through.

I turned and the two arches were there once more, so I would be able to return "Back to the Future", as Marty McFly might say. I swam through the left hand archway and was immediately struck by the sunshine. I was also surprised by the number of people in the water, which was many more than there had been in the 1950s.

I looked up and could see the cafe up the steps and also by the types of craft on the water I could tell that I had travelled forward in time once more.

Despite my earlier tiredness, I found the way back to the shore easier than I had on the way out to the archway and I was soon clambering out onto the beach once more. For some reason a few people glanced my way as I walked by and tended to stare a little bit too long.

I wondered what was wrong with me. *I wasn't naked was I?* I looked down at my body and could see that I was not naked but I was wearing a 1950s style swimming costume which looked somewhat out of place in this modern age. It was then that I noticed something else. My body was not that of a woman in her seventies, but one of a much younger woman. My breasts, while not at their absolute best, were relatively pert and slightly proud, my legs were firm and also hairless (something that I had been less worried about as a septuagenarian in the 50s).

I looked around me and the people were in dresses and outfits that fitted the 2020s. Had I spent all that time in the past and now returned to the same day as if nothing had happened?

I knew that when I had travelled back before, no time had passed here, but what I did not know was that I would not age either, as I had previously spent so little time away.

I went to check and sure enough, there were my things on the rocks. I had even left my car keys in the bag, so I got changed and wandered back up the hill. Yes, my car was there and somewhat in a daze I went to drive away. I did briefly think about going to look at Elm House to see how it had changed but I did not have the strength of character to do that then, it would be too hurtful. Instead I decided to head back to Suze's house.

CHAPTER FIFTY

11th June 2021 - Dawlish

The next morning I woke late as I had not slept well, I was back in Suze's spare room but it was now unfamiliar and not what I was used to.

The elation of the previous day had now dissipated as although I was young(ish) again, I was also homeless, penniless and alone. Plus the man I have loved for the past 32 years, had left me destitute.

Suze knew nothing of this of course and how could I explain it to her and others?

We sat quietly over breakfast, I played with my food and she noticed my grumpy disposition.

"What's up with you today?"

"Oh I'm just fed up with it all. I'm fed up of being screwed by men..." I paused, "and not in a good way!" I added before she made the obvious joke.

"I'm sure things will turn around soon Liv, you'll find a nice man, fall in love and live happily after after." She smiled one of her smiles before adding wickedly "If not, we will find you a good woman to fall in love with!" and she gave me a little wink.

At least that made me smile.

We finished breakfast and were drinking a fresh cup of coffee when the doorbell went. Suze got up and answered the door, before shouting back to me “Liv, it’s for you!”

I walked through the doorway and Suze stood aside to show a smartly dressed middle aged woman standing there.

“Olivia Jane Wylde?” she asked.

“Yes,” I answered.

“Do you have any photo ID to show that?” she enquired.

“Umm why?”

She held out a business card “My name is Lynsey Tuck from Veysey Tuck Solicitors in town.”

I knew the company name well, they were quite a large, well known firm of solicitors in South Devon.

She continued, “I've been asked to get in touch with you, with some information you might be interested in but I need to verify your identity first, if you don't mind.”

“Of course, just a minute, my driving licence is upstairs.” I dashed up to the bedroom and retrieved my driving licence from the bedside table. I wasn't quite sure why I ran up the stairs, so I took it more sedately on the way back down again.

Lynsey checked my driving licence and asked my permission before taking a photo of it. “That's fantastic. In that case I would like to ask you to join me on a short journey to a location where I might be able to enlighten you to what this is all about.”

I looked blankly at her and then looked at Suze who shrugged.

Lynsey continued, “in light of the current pandemic situation and also the fact that you don't really know me, can I suggest that I lead in my car and you follow in your car. You’re welcome to bring your friend too.”

“Where are we going?” I asked.

"I am afraid I am not at liberty to divulge that yet but it's only about a twenty minute drive away, so it won't take much time out of your day."

I looked at Suze again, once more she shrugged but this time she headed inside and got her car keys, jingling them in front of my face.

"Shall we go?" Asked Lynsey and not waiting for an answer, turned on her heels and walked towards a fairly new BMW parked on the road. I quickly got my shoes on and, shutting the door behind me, headed towards Suze's car. We headed out of town, through Teignmouth and across the Shaldon bridge.

We carried on up the hill heading towards Torquay and after a while, suspicion fell upon me. *Oh god, were we heading to Lemoncombe?*

Surely there wasn't anything else I had done wrong? Was I going to be blamed for something that had happened there or be culpable for the maintenance or something? My mind went haywire.

Suze, of course, was totally unaware of my panic and kept up a bit of commentary as we drove along "looks like we're heading to Torquay, no wait a minute, she's taking the Lemoncombe turn off, perhaps we're going for a swim?"

Finally, when Lynsey's car turned into the driveway of Elm House, my fears were confirmed when Suze said "blimey, we're heading to that old house. Bugger, this isn't anything to do with parking is it?"

We pulled up alongside Lynsey's BMW and she waited for us to get out before beckoning us to follow her into the house.

Of course to me it was only two days since I had last been there but in real time it was nearly seventy years.

I was astonished to see that so little had changed. There was some new electric lighting in the hallway but all the furniture was still the same.

"Please wait here." said Lynsey and she disappeared into what I knew was the parlour. She returned just seconds later with an envelope in her hand and presented it to me.

On the front was written "Olivia Jane Wylde". My hands shook as I held it and Suze looked over my shoulder quizzically.

The envelope opened easily despite my shaking hands and I took out the paper inside. On opening up the writing paper I recognised the handwriting almost immediately and my hands shook even more.

Lynsey then spoke " My Grandfather, John Tuck, was given that envelope in 1953 with the express instructions that a lady called Olivia Jane Wylde be tracked down and brought on this very day to this very house and given the letter to read."

Suze continued to look at me, the letter and Lynsey, as if she thought we were all mad.

"It's from Bert," I said quietly.

"Bertrand Reginald Windyett?" Asked Lynsey.

"Yes," I said.

Suze's frown deepened but I ignored them all and started to read.

"My Dear Olivia

If my plans and hopes have succeeded, then you would have returned to 2021, have become young once more and be reading this letter in our hallway.

I am sorry to have deceived you, my love, but I know that if I had told you the truth, you would not have tried to return out of some sentimentality or misguided need to stay.

By taking everything away from you, I forced you to return back to your own time and life, so you can live once more.

Elm House is yours, the deeds have been signed over in your name and my solicitor will give you the keys once you have finished reading this letter.

I have left a reasonable sum of money to ensure that the house and gardens are maintained on a regular basis so that you will not be left with a crumbling wreck in no suitable condition to live in.

My dearest, loveliest Olivia, you have made the last thirty years the happiest a man could ever expect and I now give you a gift to ensure that your next years could be as enjoyable as the days you spent with me.

I loved you from the first moment I saw you on the beach and just wish there was more I could do to ensure your happiness.

Your faithful, loving husband

Bert"

I held out the letter and cried. Lynsey had disappeared once more and this time returned with three champagne glasses on a tray which she proffered to Suze and I.

We each took a glass and as we chinked them together, Lynsey handed me a set of keys saying, "Elm House is now yours, Olivia."

"Thank you Bert," I said, raising my glass once more.

EPILOGUE

Sunday 28th November 2021 – Lemoncombe Beach

We'd had a lovely swim down at the beach and the ladies returned back to my house to relax and recuperate after the cold water.

My house. Thanks to Bert, I had my own home, a regular income from the properties he owned and the capital they'd been generating for the past sixty plus years. I was even able to work for free for a couple of charities doing Bowen therapy on sick and injured horses and dogs.

Everyone showered and I made tea and brought out scones, cream and jam. I remembered telling Bert about the battles between the Cornish and the Devonshire folk about the cream and jam order and I smiled once more.

Everything was good.I didn't have any need to fall in love again, my time with Bert was perfect and that hole was too big to fill, so I had my memories and my friends and that made me happy. My home was good. My friends were good. Our swimming was good. My life was now great!

IF YOU ENJOYED THIS BOOK, PLEASE REVIEW IT ON AMAZON BOOKS.

ISBN: 9798354786428
First Published 2022.
First Edition.

Author photo by Poppy Jakes
Copy Editing by Becky Jones

Printed in Great Britain
by Amazon

86869385R00139